shug

jenny han

ALADDIN MIX
NEW YORK   LONDON   TORONTO   SYDNEY

ALADDIN MIX
Simon & Schuster Children's Publishing Division
1230 Avenue of the Americas, New York, NY 10020
Copyright © 2006 by Jenny Han
All rights reserved, including the right of reproduction
in whole or in part in any form.
ALADDIN PAPERBACKS, ALADDIN MIX, and related logo are
registered trademarks of Simon & Schuster, Inc.
Also available in a Simon & Schuster Books for Young Readers hardcover edition.
Designed by Michael Nagin
The text of this book was set in Abobe Caslon Pro.
Manufactured in the United States of America
First Aladdin Paperbacks edition October 2007
8 10 9 7
The Library of Congress has cataloged the hardcover edition as follows:
Han, Jenny.
Shug / by Jenny Han. — 1st ed.
p. cm.
Summary: A twelve-year-old girl learns about friendship, first loves,
and self-worth in a small town in the South.
[1. Friendship—Fiction. 2. Self-esteem—Fiction.] I. Title.
PZ7.H18944Shu 2006   [Fic]—dc22
2005009367
ISBN-13: 978-1-4169-0942-2 (hc.)
ISBN-10: 1-4169-0942-7 (hc.)
ISBN-13: 978-1-4169-0943-9 (pbk.)
ISBN-10: 1-4169-0943-5 (pbk.)

0711 OFF

For Mom, Dad, Grandma, and Baby Sister

acknowledgments

I feel like a lucky star has lit my way and led me to so many amazing people, people who have been more than kind to me.

First, the Pippin women, Emily van Beek and Holly McGhee, the sexiest, cleverest, fiercest women in the business. Truly, you two are the best agents anyone could hope for. Next, my editor, Emily Thomas, for holding my hand and for being Annemarie's surrogate mama. You've done right by her and by me, Emily. Thank you to Michael Nagin for the sweetest cover ever, and to Dorothy Gribbin, Chava Wolin, and the whole S&S family for getting behind *Shug*. I also thank Sarah Weeks, my friend and mentor—you have been nothing but generous with me, and if it hadn't been for you, none of this would be possible. And who could forget David Levithan, who has counseled me tirelessly and who also shares my deep and abiding affection for all things Angela Chase and BSC. Also a shout-out to the Writing for Children kids at the New School and especially to my writing group: Melinda, Emmy, Lisa, and Caroline. Write on, ladies. You are all so very exquisite. Thank you also to the Claires—Holly, John, Foster, and Claire: Thank you for being my home away from home and for allowing me to be a part of your family. You are so dear to me.

Lastly, I'd like to thank all my friends and family for cheering me on and especially B, *ma soeur d'ame*, and Sarah Elizabeth, who's been there since the beginning.

chapter 1

It is the end of a summer afternoon and the sun will be setting soon, our favorite part of the day. We're eating Popsicles, cherry ones. My shirt is sticking to my back, and my hands feel sugary and warm, but my lips are cool. The sun is turning that fiery pink I love, and I turn to Mark the way I always do.

I look at him, really look at him. We have sat under this tree, our tree, a hundred times or more, and he's always been the same Mark—the Mark I have known since we were five years old and I told him my mama was a whole lot prettier than his. But today, at this very moment, he is different, and it's not even something I can explain. But I feel it. Boy, do I feel it. On the outside, everything looks the way it always does, but on the inside, it's like some little part of me is waking up.

His hair is hanging in his eyes, and his skin is brown as toast. He smells the way he always smells in summer—like green grass and sweat and chlorine. He's watching the sun turn its different colors, and he's all quiet and hushed up. He turns to me and smiles, and in that moment he is so dear to me I hurt inside. That's when I feel it—like my heart might burst right out of my chest. This is it; this is the exact moment when he is supposed to kiss me, the kind of moment movies are made for. He'll look at me, and he'll know, just like I know.

Everybody knows that twelve is the perfect age for your first kiss.

Except, he isn't looking at me anymore. And he's talking; the big jerk is talking when he should be kissing. He's going on about some mountain bike his dad is going to buy him for his birthday. "Man, it's gonna be sweet. We're gonna go on the Tuckashawnee trail—"

"Hey, Mark," I interrupt. I'm giving him one last chance to make this moment up to me, one last chance to see me the way I see him. I will him to look at me, really *look* at me. Don't see the mosquito bites on my legs, don't see the ketchup stain on my shorts, or the scabs on my elbows.

Don't see the girl you've known your whole life. See me. *See me.*

"Yeah?" He's looking at me, and he doesn't see me at all. I can tell he's still thinking about that bike and hasn't even thought of kissing me. His mouth is cherry red from his Popsicle. He looks like he's wearing lipstick.

"You look like you're wearing lipstick," I say. "You look like a girl. A girl with really bad taste." I laugh like it's the funniest thing in the world.

He flushes. "Shut up, Annemarie," he says, wiping away at his mouth furiously.

"I bet Celia has some eye shadow that would look terrif with that lipstick," I continue. Celia is my big sister, and probably the prettiest girl in our town, maybe even the state.

Mark glares at me. "You're just jealous because Celia's prettier than you."

I bite my lip. "You should let Celia give you a makeover," I say. My eyes are starting to burn. When the two of us get started we don't quit until one of us leaves crying. Usually it's Mark, but this time I am afraid it will be me.

Please, please don't let it be me.

"You're the one who could use a makeover," Mark says cruelly.

"You are really ignorant, Mark, you know that? You're a real troglodyte. You're so ignorant, I bet you don't even know what that means." It means a primitive person who lives in caves. I only know because I looked it up after Celia called me one when I tried to eat grapes with my toes.

"So what? I bet you don't know what it means either. I bet you copied it off your mom or your sister."

"I did not. I happen to be gifted. I never copy off of anybody, unlike some troglodytes I know."

Last year I caught Mark copying Jack Connelly's homework on the bus. He pretended like it was no big deal in front of his buddies, but when I threatened to tell his mama, Mrs. Findley, he started boohooing like a little baby. The dumbest part is that Jack Connelly is easily the least smart person in our grade. If Mark's a troglodyte, Jack is king of the troglodytes.

Mark gapes at me and shakes his head disgustedly. "Geez, Annemarie, why'd you have to bring that up? You started it."

"I was just foolin', and if you weren't so dense, you'd know better than to criticize a girl's looks. It's degrading, and it's, well, it's sexist." I raise my eyebrows high and dare him to disagree.

"What a load of crap. You can say whatever you want

to me, and I can't say jack to you?" Mark says, shaking his head again. "That's dumb."

"That's the way it goes," I say. "And anyway, you didn't have to rub it in about Celia. I know she's prettier than me."

My sister Celia is the kind of girl whose hair curls just right in a ponytail. She is smaller than me, the kind of small that boys want to scoop up and hold on to real tight. I am too tall for even my daddy to scoop up anymore, much less a sixth grade boy. Boys like Celia; they go crazy for her sneaky smiles and sassy strut. They are always calling the house and making Daddy frown. Mama just smiles and says, "the boys buzz around my Celia because they know she is sweeter than honey." I sure wish boys would buzz around me.

On every Valentine's Day since the fourth grade, Celia has come home with pink carnations and solid milk chocolate hearts and at least one Whitman's Sampler. She always lets me eat the square ones with caramel inside, even though they are her favorite too. The most I ever get on Valentine's Day are the valentines the class got for one another because they had to, the Scooby-Doo or Mickey Mouse kind that come twenty-four to a box at the drugstore.

Mark gives me his "I'm sorry" look—his half grin–half grimace that's supposed to look like real remorse. He looks like he always does when he has messed up, like a puppy that's peed on himself and is sorry, but will inevitably do it again. Mark Findley has been saying sorry to me his whole life.

"Sorry, Annemarie," he says.

I scowl at him. "Yeah, well, you should be."

He's still giving me The Look, and then he gets on his knees. "Forgive me, Annemarie! Please, please forgive me!" he begs, swaying back and forth with his hands clasped in prayer.

He is so dumb.

The thing I hate worst about Mark is that I can never, ever stay mad at him. I can hold a grudge better than anybody I know, but with Mark it is truly impossible. He always finds a way to make me laugh.

"Oh, get up." Trying to hide my smile, I tear a handful of grass out of the ground and throw it at his head.

He sees the smile that got away and looks satisfied. Then he shakes the grass out of his hair the way my dog Meeks does after a bath. "Where is Celia, anyway?" Mark asks oh-so-casually, falling back onto the ground.

Mark has had a crush on Celia since we were little kids. He's never said so, but he doesn't have to. He knows I know.

"She's at the mall with Margaret Tolliver, and then they're having a sleepover at Margaret's house." Margaret Tolliver is Celia's best friend, and sometimes they let me come along. Today was not one of those times.

"Oh," he says. It hurts to hear so much disappointment in that one little word and I know he still likes her. Celia's sixteen, and we're twelve, so you'd think Mark would know he doesn't have a prayer. And I guess he does know, but he still hopes. Next to the high school guys that like Celia, Mark looks like a little kid. I guess he knows that too. But he still follows Celia around the same way old Meeks does when he's hoping for scraps.

We don't say anything for a minute; we just watch the sun disappear. Then Mark stands up. "I guess I'd better go home," he says. "You wanna come over for dinner? I think Mom's making spaghetti tonight."

Mrs. Findley's spaghetti is the Best Ever, capital *B*, capital *E*. She makes the sauce from scratch and everything—roasted tomatoes, fresh basil from her garden, sweet Italian sausage. Her secret ingredient is honey; it adds a sweetness to the sauce. Mrs. Findley's spaghetti is my favorite. I know this is Mark's way of making it up to me, and I want to say yes, but instead I say, "Nah, Mama's probably already fixed somethin' special for me."

This is a bald-faced lie, and we both know it. Mama hates to cook, and the only time she ever really bothers is when my daddy is at home. Daddy is in Atlanta on business for another week, so the best I can hope for is a peanut butter sandwich. And that's only if Celia bought bread today.

But I sure as heck won't admit any of that to Mark. I'll probably be dining on Extra Crunchy Jif tonight, but at least I won't have shamed my mama. Not that she would even be ashamed, but I know for a fact that she doesn't like the neighborhood knowing our family business. Mama's big on pride. She's always telling me that a woman without pride is no woman at all. I know that I'm not a woman in the places that really count, but I can at least get the pride part right.

Mark shrugs, and says, "Are you gonna go to Sherilyn's pool party next Saturday?"

"Yup." Our friend Sherilyn Tallini has a pool party at the end of every summer, right before school starts. It used to be typical kid stuff—hot dogs and Sharks and Minnows and neighborhood moms wearing one-pieces with terry cloth cover-ups and matching terry cloth slippers. All except for Sherylin's mom, who only wears string bikinis with maybe a sarong. All the other mothers smile and pretend to like Mrs. Tallini, but really they think she is "attractive in a used up, tanning bed kind of way." I know because I heard Mairi Stevenson's mom say it at the Fourth of July parade last year.

Mrs. Tallini does have a tanning bed but, as I've heard my daddy say, she is "still one good-lookin' woman." If my mother heard him say this, she would skin him good, but fortunately for us all, Mama does not attend neighborhood functions.

I know what the other mothers think of Mama. They think she is stuck-up and pretentious. They think she thinks she is better than they are. And it's true; she does. My mother, Grace, is very tall and very beautiful in an intimidating sort of way, the kind of way that says she knows it but doesn't give a hoot. Mama's hair is the color of wheat, the kind that gleams red and gold in the sunlight, and her eyes are dark green. My daddy calls her Grace Kelly, which Mama turns her nose up at because according to her, it's far too conventional, but I know she secretly enjoys it. She says that Daddy is no prince, and if she's gonna be compared to anyone, it had better be Lauren Bacall.

Daddy thinks that Mama is everything a woman should be: beautiful, clever, charming. Beauty has a way of making the bad things tolerable. When Mama tilts her green eyes at you, it's hard to remember why you were mad in the first place. That's her special gift.

My mother is unlike every other mother in our neighborhood—she went to college up North, and she had the nerve to come back "all citified, puttin' on airs like she's Princess Diana." (If you're wondering how I know all this, it's because adults think that kids can't play and listen at the same time.) Mama grew up with a lot of the other mothers in our town, and you can just bet they were smug when she had to come back home.

Mama reads Foucault, not Danielle Steel, and she makes martinis, not green bean casserole. In the kitchen, there are poetry books where the cookbooks should be, and she doesn't have a dish towel with mallard ducks on it or a ceramic magnet that says "Home Sweet Home" on our refrigerator. Mama is always telling Celia and me that we are worth twelve of this town, and that she'll disinherit us if we don't leave as soon as we graduate high school. Mama is halfheartedly invited to neighborhood parties like the Tallini's, but she never fails to graciously decline and the other mothers never fail to be relieved.

Last year was the first year Sherilyn's pool party was different. None of the other mothers were there, and Mrs.

Tallini only came outside to serve lunch. I ate two pieces of fried chicken as opposed to my standard four, because none of the other girls were eating anything. We didn't play Sharks and Minnows, and all the other girls wore two-piece bathing suits and lay on deck chairs while the boys tried to splash them. I was the only one who wore the same one-piece bathing suit I had worn the year before. I told the other girls it was because I think bikinis are offensive and degrading to women, so I guess that means I'm stuck wearing my one-piece again this year.

"You wanna walk over to Sherilyn's together?" Mark asks.

"Yeah, okay," I say.

"Okay, then, see you later." He pauses. "And, Annemarie, sorry about what I said before. I didn't mean it."

He meant it. Some girls are pretty, and it's like they were destined for it. They were meant to be pretty, and as for the rest of us, well, we get to exist on the outer edges of life. It's like moths. They're the same as butterflies, aren't they? They're just gray. They can't help being gray, they just are. But butterflies, they're a million different colors, yellow and emerald and cerulean blue. They're pretty. Who'd dare kill a butterfly? I don't know of a single soul who'd lift a finger against a butterfly. But most anybody would swat at a moth like it was nothing, and all because it isn't pretty. Doesn't seem fair, not at all.

Mark heads for home, and I watch him go, feeling the lump in my throat grow. I never knew love felt like cancer of the throat. Before he turns the corner, he waves and I wave back.

It's not like I've never liked a boy before. There was Sherwood Brown, who I met at camp last June. He was staying with his grandma all summer, and we smiled at each other every day at camp. He and his friends would splash me and my friends in the pool, and sometimes he even sat next to me on the bus when we went on day trips. When I told him I liked him, he said he kind of liked me too, but his grandma would whup him good if he ever brought home a white girl. I went home and told Mama, and she laughed until tears ran down her face. She said Sherwood Brown had better learn to stand up to his grandma, or he'd be a little girl his whole life. I decided then and there that I wouldn't be talking to Mama about boys, not ever.

And of course there was Kyle Montgomery, the best-looking boy in our grade. All the girls like Kyle Montgomery. Even the teachers like Kyle. Us girls pretend-swoon when we see him in the hallways. The one time he caught my best friend Elaine Kim and me doing it, he winked at us, and then he turned bright red. We like Kyle because he's out of our league; he's out of everybody's league. Plus he's fun to giggle about. I don't know of any girl who wouldn't die for a chance to walk down the hallway with Kyle Montgomery.

Kyle Montgomery is tall, and he has nice eyes. You know the kind of eyes that always look like they're smiling? Well, Kyle has them, and he really does smile an awful lot. His jeans always fit just right, and he is the best basketball player our school has ever seen. So like I said, everyone likes Kyle, and I did my fair share of liking him too a few years back.

But this is different; this is Mark. This is Mark Findley who knows my favorite ice cream flavor (Rocky Road) and how I like my pizza (extra cheese, pineapple, and mushroom); Mark who pulls splinters out of my feet when I go barefoot in the summer; Mark who helped me bury my gerbil, Benny, when he died. This is Mark who was sitting next to me on the bus that time I threw up in third grade. He didn't even say a word when some splashed on him; he just wiped it off and asked me if I was okay.

One of the things I like best about Mark is his family. The Findleys are the kind of family you only see on black-and-white reruns late at night. At Christmastime,

Mrs. Findley makes cinnamon cookies out of piecrust and real whipped cream to put on top, and Mr. Findley used to take Mark and Celia and me sledding at Clementon Park. (This was before Celia decided she was too grown up to have fun.) Mrs. Findley always says that she wishes she had a daughter just like me, and that my mother is the luckiest woman alive for having *two* lovely daughters. Mrs. Findley thinks I am lovely. When we were little, I secretly wanted the Findleys to adopt me, but now that I'm older, I suppose I would settle for being their cherished daughter-in-law.

chapter 2

When I get home, I go straight to my bedroom and call Elaine. Elaine Kim moved to our neighborhood last December. Everyone wanted to be her best friend because she was new and from New York City, but she chose me.

I say, "Elaine, I have some news."

"What?" she says, and I can hear the TV in the background.

I pause. "I think I'm in love . . . with Mark."

"Yeah, I know," Elaine says. I can tell she is watching TV and not paying attention to me, and I am annoyed.

"I said, I think I'm in love with Mark," I snap.

"I said, I know!" Elaine snaps right back. I love that about her.

"How did you know? You couldn't have known. I didn't even know."

"Come on, Annemarie. I'm your best friend. I know stuff about you that nobody knows, not even you."

"But *how* did you know?"

"Because it's a total cliché; of course you like Mark. He's the boy next door, the boy you'll measure every other boy against. It was only a matter of time." Just because Elaine's father is a psychiatrist, she thinks she knows everything.

"Mark doesn't live next door," I mutter.

"Down the street, whatever. Same thing."

"Okay fine, if you know so much, what am I going to do about it?"

"What are you going to do?" she repeats. "I don't know. What do you want to do?"

"I want him to like me back. I want him to look at me the way he looks at Celia," I say, lying back on my pillow and staring at the ceiling. There is a massive spiderweb in one corner.

"Hmm, that could be hard. Celia has, like, actual breasts, remember?"

"No, I forgot, but thank you for reminding me."

Elaine decides that I should talk to my mother. According to her, while other mothers are clueless, mine understands these sorts of things. Elaine idolizes my mother, maybe because hers is so unlike mine. She is the only one of my friends Mama can stand, because she is from New York and because Mama thinks she has "moxie." But I think it's because Elaine acts like Mama is a movie star, and Mama loves it when people are smart enough to know she is something special.

I know better than to ask Mama about Mark because I know exactly what she will say. She will say that Mark is sweet in a prosaic sort of way, but I can do better because I am extraordinary. And then I'll start to think that maybe Mark really is sort of prosaic, and I'll never be able to see him in the same way ever again.

I don't tell Elaine this though. I like the way Elaine looks at Mama. I wish I still looked at Mama that way. Sometimes I do, but it's getting harder and harder.

Even though Mama messed up that one time I told her about Sherwood Brown, that doesn't mean she won't come through this time. You never know. People can surprise you. And I mean, life is all about second chances, right?

After Elaine and I hang up, I go to Mama's room.

My mother is reading in bed, with her feet propped up on a silk pillow. It is turquoise with little orange tassels. "Shug, don't slouch," she says, not lifting her eyes from the page.

I roll my eyes and sit on the edge of the bed, at her feet.

"Mama, when's dinner?" I ask. I know full well she hasn't cooked any.

She looks up, surprised. "You know your daddy's away on business, and your sister's at Margaret's, so I didn't bother with dinner. You fix something up for yourself; I'm not hungry."

"Mama!"

"What?" she says absentmindedly. She reaches for the wineglass on her nightstand and turns the page of her book.

"Mama, I need to talk to you. I need some advice."

Mama takes a long sip of wine. "Okay, Shug," she says. "You have my complete and undivided attention. What's going on?"

"Well, the thing is, I like someone. A boy," I say. "But I don't think he likes me."

Mama nods. "Who is this boy?"

I hesitate. "Mama, you can't tell anyone."

"All right."

"You have to promise, Mama."

"I promise. I shan't tell a soul." She crosses her heart.

"Well, okay. It's Mark." I watch her hopefully.

Mama finishes her wine, and says, "Mark Findley . . . Hmm . . . yes, he is a charming boy."

Hope begins to flutter in my chest like a little bird. See, all she needed was that second chance. Mama knows all about men, maybe she really could help me decide what to do.

"But, Shug, I sure hope your babies take after our side of the family and not his. His mama is just as common as coal." She winks at me and goes back to her book.

Sometimes I hate my mother so much I can't breathe.

"At least Mrs. Findley makes dinner," I spit out.

"Why, Miss Annemarie, are you mad at me?" She's mocking me, and it only makes me madder.

"You're just jealous of Mrs. Findley; that's why you say ugly things about her. And coal isn't common. It's a precious resource."

"Shug, I was only joking. You know I've always been fond of Mark, and I think his mama is really very sweet," Mama says. "If you want Mark, you go and get him. I didn't raise my daughters to be pacifists. Make love or make war, Shug, but make somethin' happen. And you've got hands; you can fix your own dinner."

"Fine!" I leap off the bed and storm out.

As I stomp down the stairs, as loudly as bare feet on carpet will allow, I hear my mother call, "Love you too, baby mine."

My mother has never forgiven Mrs. Findley for being the kind of mother I have always wished for.

chapter 3

Elaine once asked me why Mama calls me Shug. I said, "Have you ever read *The Color Purple*?" She said no, and I said, "Well there's this character named Shug, Shug Avery . . ." I tried to explain, but I guess I didn't do a very good job because she looked at me like I was crazy.

So I said, "Never mind. It's just Shug, Shug like sugar."

The Color Purple is one of Mama's favorite books. Mine too. It's all about living free, on the inside. The main character's name is Celie (like Celia, see) and she's had a real beat-down kind of life. She thinks she's nothing. Then Celie meets Shug Avery, and boy, is Shug Avery a force of nature. That's what Mama calls her, anyway. Shug Avery doesn't take crap from nothin' and nobody. She's a singer and a temptress, too. When Shug Avery blows through town, she shakes the whole town up. Everyone's enchanted by her: Celie, Celie's husband, Mr. ____ ; everyone. My mama, too.

That's why she calls me Shug—well, that, and it's short for sugar. Plenty of mamas call their babies Shug, but for Mama, I know it's more than a sweet way of talking. She wants me to be like Shug Avery, to squeeze every last drop out of life and be special, the way she and Shug are. And to be beautiful, the way she and Shug are. I think Mama's still waiting for that part, for me to grow up and be beautiful. I think she might be waiting for that part forever.

It's ironic, because Celia's already beautiful, and she was the one named for Celie, the plainest girl alive. I think maybe I should've been named Celie. Instead I am Annemarie, named for Mama's sister who died when she was little. Mama says she was somethin' special, wild and freer than anybody Mama knew. That must be pretty darn free.

I think that first Annemarie would've been worthy of a name like Shug. Not me, though. I'm like Miss Celie on the inside, scared of everything. But in the end, even that old scaredycat Celie finds out how to live, how to *be*. She shows everybody what she can do; she shows them all. I want that too.

chapter 4

Celia comes home early the next morning and goes straight to bed. She is always cranky after a sleepover with Margaret, and then she sleeps till noon. When she finally emerges, I am sitting at the kitchen table, reading.

Our kitchen is one of my favorite places in the whole house. There are lots of windows, and the sun shines through all day. Mama has Marc Chagall prints on the wall. They used to scare me, but I have come to admire them.

"Hey, Shug. Where's Mama?" Celia asks, pouring herself a glass of orange juice. She rumples my hair and sits across from me.

"She went to the art museum with Gail," I say, taking

her juice before she can have the first sip. Gail is Mama's friend from work. Mama is the part-time activities director at the Rosemont Retirement Community, and Gail is one of the nurses.

Celia snatches it right back. She drinks some, and hands it back to me.

"What did you and Margaret do?" I ask, finishing the glass.

"We just hung out with some of the guys," Celia says vaguely. "You want lunch?"

I say yes, and Celia cooks us cheddar omelets and bacon. As we eat, I watch her and think about how much she looks like Daddy. She has Mama's green eyes, but the rest of her is all Daddy. Her hair is soft and brown like a puppy's, and she has Daddy's smile. Her hair hangs down her back in soft curls, and she is wearing her old Snoopy T-shirt. I'm so busy thinking how pretty she is that I almost forget to tell her my big news.

My mouth full of bacon, I say, "Celia, guess what."

"What? And don't talk with your mouth full; it's gross."

I open my mouth wider and stick my tongue out, bacon bits and all. Celia shakes her head in disgust. "I like someone," I say.

"Who?"

And then, in that moment, I know I can't tell Celia. Not this time. Not before I get him, and not until he's mine.

The lie comes out before I even have time to think it through. "Kyle Montgomery."

"Kyle? Didn't you have a crush on him in fourth grade? I thought you were over Kyle."

"Yeah, but that was kid stuff. I didn't really know what love was back then. This is the real thing," I say. It is the real thing too. It's as real as anything I've ever felt, and when I am old, people might try and tell me different, I might even tell myself different, but I know that at this moment, I love Mark Findley.

"I see him in a whole new way now. I see him . . . as the boy he is today, and the man he will one day be."

Celia laughs. "You're still such a kid, Shug. What you're feeling right now is just puppy love. But don't worry: Kyle's sweet. He'll make a good first boyfriend."

Ha! What does she know? Celia, who's had more boyfriends than I've had socks. She doesn't know the first thing about true love.

"First of all, I'm not a kid anymore," I say coldly, ignoring Celia's smirk. "And second of all, that's the whole problem, Miss Expert on Love, always thinking you know everything! He doesn't like me."

"Why not?"

"He likes someone else."

Celia's eyes narrow, and she looks just like Mama. "Who?"

"Just some girl at school," I say. "She's a bit more womanly than me."

Celia snorts. "You, Shug? A woman?" She throws her head back and laughs like one of those crazy hyenas from *The Lion King*.

I glare at her. "Oh ha ha ha, poor pathetic Shug. I come to you for advice about this—this harpy, and this is what I get." We learned about harpies during the Greek mythology unit at school last year. Harpies were monsters who were part woman, part bird, and they had talons and they would shriek and laugh at people. Sounds like Celia to me.

"Look, Annemarie," Celia says, sighing. "Forget about this other girl and worry about yourself, if you really want to be a contender. You've got to get in the game before you can knock out your opponent. So quit feeling sorry for yourself, dummy. Take action. Do yourself up; flirt with his friends. Make him notice you. Make him *work* for it."

"Will that really work?"

"'Course it will, Shuggy Pie. It works every time. Boys

25

are essentially all the same. They need you to do the think-ing for them. Trust me, he'll come around," she says confi-dently. "You're not bad lookin', even if you are a pain most of the time." Celia sticks her plate in the sink and says she's going to the lake with Margaret and Kristi and Jake and everybody.

I hope she'll invite me, but she doesn't.

After Celia leaves, I call up Elaine. Nobody answers, so I call Mark next.

"Hey," I say. "What are you doing?"

"Some of the guys are over here," Mark says.

"Like who?"

"Just some of the guys—Jack and Kyle and Tommy."

Ha! My first big chance to make Mark notice me, make him see me for the woman I am! I'll make the whole room notice me! I'll be the femme fatale I was born to be! I can see it now: me, slinking around the Findley's rec room like a real temptress, the boys, hovering around me like nerv-ous little bees, eager to do my bidding.

"What are you guys doing?" I say, real casual-like.

"I don't know. Just hangin' out, playing video games and stuff," Mark says distractedly.

"Can I come over?"

"If you want."

"Okay, well, maybe I will," I say. He says okay, and we hang up.

I put my dishes in the sink and go to my room. I've been to Mark's house a million times or more and not once have I thought about what I was wearing. But there are going to be *guys* over there, not to mention this new Mark. And if I am going to be the femme fatale, I've got to look the part.

I look in the mirror, and I am sorry to see it's still just me there. Who was I trying to kid? I'm no femme fatale. I'm not the kind of girl boys like.

My hair is a lighter, less special version of my mother's. It's like dirty straw: There are no reds or golds, and it's too fine to curl the way Celia's does. It just sits at my shoulders and hangs. Elaine's hair is long and coffee black, and I envy the dark richness of it, mine being just a pale imitation of someone else's hair. My eyes are brown, the muddy kind of brown you get when you mix a bunch of watercolors together. My body is bony and stickstraight, not soft and curvy like Celia's. I am tall, too tall for my age, and I have no womanly curves to speak of. I can't fill a pudding cup with what I've got. But worst of all are my freckles. I have freckles scattered all over me, like sprinkles on a crummy cake no one feels like eating. No one else in my family has freckles.

I wonder if I'll ever be pretty. Probably not. Not Mama and Celia's kind of pretty, anyway. Daddy says I am like a baby colt, and that one day, I will be a real knockout. Don't fathers know that you're not supposed to say, *One day you will be a knockout*? Don't they know that you're supposed to say, *You are a knockout right this very minute, just the way you are*? Daddy's just as bad as Mark; neither of them ever know how to say the right thing.

But Celia said I wasn't bad lookin', and that's something. Maybe "not bad" is good enough for Mark to like. Anyway, it's not like he's some prize. His feet smell like nachos half the time, and Mrs. Findley always cuts his hair too short in the back. Still, he's Mark, and he's mine.

Mama said to make love or make war. I know she doesn't mean I should go and have sexual relations with him, but that's about all I know. Should I just forget the femme fatale stuff and tell him that I am in love with him, and that he should love me too, or else? Or should I be coy like Celia said, and make him wildly jealous so he'll come chasing after me? I knew Mama wouldn't be any help. Come to think of it, neither was Celia.

chapter 5

When you walk into Mark's house, you are overcome with the notion that a real family lives there. Family portraits are lovingly hung on every wall, and Mark's school pictures have the seat of honor above the fireplace. The one from second grade is my personal favorite. He's missing one of his front teeth, and his hair is slicked to the side like a used car salesman.

There are little baskets of potpourri all over the place, and Mrs. Findley's ceramic teapot collection is displayed throughout the house. And it always smells the same, like pumpkin pie and fresh laundry. It smells the way a house should smell—warm and good and safe.

I walk right through the front door because I'm

practically a part of the family. Mrs. Findley is icing a red velvet cake in the kitchen. My favorite.

"Hi, Mrs. Findley," I say.

"Hello, dear. I've made cream cheese icing, just the way you and Mark like it, extra sweet." She gives me her special smile, the one where her nose wrinkles.

"Thanks, Mrs. Findley."

She sprinkles a handful of chopped pecans on top of the cake and says, "Sit with me a minute and chat, Annemarie."

So I do. Talking to Mrs. Findley is as easy as talking to Elaine or Celia, but in a different way. She listens and nods, and she makes you feel safe.

When I told Mark that my mama was a whole lot prettier than his, I was only five, so what did I know about anything? It may be true that Mama's prettier, but Mrs. Findley has a warm kind of beauty few people will ever be able to fully appreciate or comprehend. It's in the way she touches people, looks at people like they're something special even when they're not.

Her hair is light brown and beginning to gray at the crown of her head. Her eyes are the color of Daddy's bourbon, wise and gentle. Mrs. Findley is a few years older than my mother, and I suppose I should mention that she is not from the South. She's from the Midwest. This may seem like a trivial detail, but somehow, it matters. She is different; she is unique.

Mark will never know how lucky he is to have been born to a lady like Mrs. Findley. People who have it that good rarely do.

I get so comfortable talking to Mrs. Findley, I sort of dread the thought of walking into a den of boys. There is something about walking into a room full of boys that makes you feel exposed and somehow all wrong. You feel inadequate, like you come up short in every way that matters. It didn't used to be like this, and I don't know when it changed, but now it feels like it was always this way.

That's why I'm relieved when Mrs. Findley suggests that I bring the cake down to the rec room. It gives me some sort of purpose, a reason to be there. Plus, it's always easier to walk into a room carrying something—a purse, a cake, a baseball bat. Anything to make you look like you belong.

The boys don't even look up when I come into the room. I am carrying the cake, and plates and forks underneath it, and when I say, "I've got cake," they finally look at me. I am wearing an old yellow sundress of Celia's, and I have tied my hair back with green ribbon. I think I look real nice. And all they see is the cake.

Mark says, "All right!" He grabs the cake and sets it on the coffee table. "Hey, where's the knife?"

I glare at him. "It's your house. You go get the knife."

That bum Jack Connelly says, "Aw, pipe down, Annemarie. You're the girl. Well, sort of." He smirks. "Girls are in charge of the food; that's the way it is and that's the way it's always gonna be. You better get used to it."

"You're a pig, you know that? Oink, oink. You just roll around in your own feces all day thinking stupid thoughts." I laugh at my own joke.

"Why don't you go home and play with your Barbies?" he snaps. "What are you doing here, anyway?"

I hate Jack Connelly.

I've hated him ever since the third grade. It was lunchtime, and this was when we still had assigned seats in the cafeteria. Jack was bragging about how he had been tested for his IQ, and the doctor had told him he had a genius IQ of 300. I told him that I knew for a fact that he didn't have an IQ of 300, that a genius IQ was 140, that Albert Einstein himself only had an IQ of 160, and besides, Jack could barely spell his own name. Jack got mad, and before I knew it, we were kicking each other's chairs, and I kicked so hard he fell out of his chair and I stubbed my toe. The cafeteria monitor yelled at us, and we both had to skip recess that day. From then on, we were sworn enemies.

Every day at school we would try to outdo each other. He told everyone that I was born with both girl and boy parts. I told everyone that his own parents had tried to sell him on the black market, but nobody would take him cause he was so ugly. Then one afternoon he tripped me on the playground, and to this very day, there is a tiny scar on my left cheek. You can barely see it anymore, but it's there, and it's all because of Jack Connelly.

We're still snarling at each other when Kyle Montgomery says, "Hey, thanks for bringing the cake down, Annemarie."

Tommy Malone says nothing. His eyes dart back to the video game that has been paused.

Mark says, "Let's eat the cake later; I wanna finish this game." Then he finally seems to notice me. "Why are you wearing a dress?"

"Because everything else was dirty. It's Celia's." My face feels hot.

He shrugs, and he and Jack and Tommy return to the TV while Kyle cuts into the cake with a fork. He cuts five lopsided pieces, and slides them onto the plates. I sit on the couch with my arms crossed and watch him silently. I wish I could think of something smart to say.

"So, who's your homeroom teacher?" Kyle asks, passing me a plate. I rest the plate at the edge of my lap to hide my scabby knees.

"Mrs. Simone. Who's yours?" I take a big bite of cake, careful not to let any crumbs fall. They do anyway.

"Same. I heard she's nice."

"Yeah."

I wish Elaine was here. When it comes to boys, Elaine is confident and supremely sure of herself. Maybe it's because she's from New York, but Elaine can flirt with the best of 'em. She acts like she's hot stuff, and everybody believes it. It's a trick of hers. I know she would have had Kyle Montgomery feeding her cake by the end of the afternoon.

Why oh why is it so much harder to talk to boys like Kyle? It's not that he isn't nice, because he is, nicer than most of the boys my age. There is just something disarming about good-looking people. They make you feel all fluttery and nervous, and you hardly know where to look. I settle on staring at a freckle under his right eye. The freckle makes me feel better, knowing that a good-looking person like Kyle Montgomery can have freckles and still be good-looking.

He asks me which honors classes I'll be taking in seventh grade, and I say all of them. I ask him if he's gonna try out for the basketball team, and he says yes. Before long, we're talking.

I lean back into the couch. This isn't so bad. Sure, I'm no femme fatale, and sure, the boys aren't swarming around me, but it's not so bad. I'm sitting next to Kyle Montgomery and I'm holding my own. I'm a woman in my own right.

We talk about Mr. Romano's honors math class, and playing softball, at which point Tommy comes and joins us on the couch. Tommy is uneasy around girls, but he likes sports well enough. So I keep the topic on sports, we eat cake, and everything is fine. I check to see if Mark has noticed, but he and Jack are too busy with their dratted game.

When Mark and Jack finally finish their game, they clamor for cake, and the atmosphere changes all over again. It's so much easier when it's just you and the one boy. It's easier to be you without a big audience.

The boys discuss the upcoming basketball season, and although I know as much about basketball as anyone else, certainly Mark, I stay silent. At moments like these, saying the wrong thing would be disaster. And anyway, it's hard to find a moment to break in with one of my snazzy witticisms. It's darn near impossible to get a word in when there are boys around. They take over everything and breathe up all the air in the room.

Mercifully, the afternoon passes by without major incident. Jack comments on my eating three pieces of cake, but Jack is a dunce, so who cares? I can't be bothered with worrying about people like Jack Connelly. When it's time to go, I am left feeling empty. I don't know what I was expecting to happen, but it sure wasn't this.

The whole time we were sitting there, my eyes kept sliding back to Mark. How is it possible to have known a boy for eight years and never have seen how special he was, how terribly, secretly wonderful? Everything about him seems special now. I can't stop looking at him, and I keep wanting to touch his hair or squeeze his hand. It's so distracting. If anyone else noticed, I'd die.

Mark didn't look at me once. I mean, he looked at me, but not once did he see me.

chapter 6

I live in the kind of town where people are always saying things like, "I can't wait to get out of here" and "When I get out of this town . . ." They usually want to move to New York, and they say those two words with real reverence: New York. It even sounds capitalized. Everybody dreams big where I am from, but nobody's dreams ever come true. New York City might as well be Never-Never Land for all the good it will do anybody from Clementon.

The thing is, you can't ever really leave Clementon. The sweet South lures you back home, just like those Sirens in Greek mythology. You might go to college somewhere else, you might even move away, but you always end up coming back. That's what happened to my mama.

She and my daddy were both born and raised in Clementon. They both went to Clementon High, they dated, and then they went their separate ways to college— Mama to a women's college up North, and Daddy to the state school. When Grandpa Cavane got sick her junior year, Mama had to come home and go to the state school too. I guess she and Daddy met up at college and it was all fireworks. They fell right back in love and got married after graduation.

It's so strange to think about what could have happened if Mama had never come back home, had never met up with Daddy again, had never gotten married. I would have a different daddy and all different genes. Maybe I'd be bite-size, with strawberry blond curls and a tiny nose. Maybe I'd have cocoa skin and mocha latte eyes with long, long lashes. And breasts. Maybe I'd be a good dancer or a gymnast or a figure skater. My potential might have known no bounds; I might have been great.

It's funny, because in all my fantasies of *What if Mama and Daddy had never,* Mama is always my mother. It's only my father that changes. I reckon it's his fault I'm ten feet tall with a bird chest and big feet. If I looked like my mama, things might be different for me.

Clementon is a small town. Everybody knows everybody,

and everybody knows everybody else's business, too. It's that kind of place. Mama thinks it's suffocating, but I like knowing that Bernard Watts's dog was just neutered, or that Emmy Jo Delessi's wedding cost her parents over twenty-five thousand dollars. (I had no idea that one day could cost so much money, but apparently her tiara was made out of real seed pearls, and they also served jumbo shrimp cocktail at the reception.) I like knowing that every fall we have our Clementon County Fair, and every Christmas we have our Clementon County Christmas Pageant. I like walking into Mr. Boneci's family diner and hearing him say, "Hey there, Miss Annemarie. Long time no see."

I'm not trying to say that there aren't plenty of negative aspects of small-town life too, because there are. There's a lot of "small town small mindedness," as Mama puts it. When Olivia Peterson got pregnant last year, she wasn't allowed to go to school anymore. I don't know if that is illegal or what, but nobody put up a fuss. Not even Olivia.

Clementon has its bad points, but I wouldn't mind living here for the rest of my life. I really wouldn't. It's home. I was born here; it's what I'm used to.

chapter 7

Last night I discovered my bathing suit had a hole in it. This may sound petty, but for a girl who has to go to a boy-girl pool party in a matter of hours, it is no small thing. It is quite a big thing, possibly the biggest. I wore that bathing suit all summer, and just when I needed it most, it fell apart on me. When I tried it on, I didn't notice at first, and then I felt the light breeze on my butt.

Mama sewed the hole up straight away. I didn't even know she could sew. I almost didn't trust her with it because she'd had half a bottle of wine with supper, but she did a good job. I was really impressed. She had the right color string and everything. You can't even tell there was a hole. It looks as good as new, or as good as a two-year-old stretched-out bathing suit can look, anyway. It's faded green, and although it's not a two-piece, it does have pretty little straps.

Midmorning Elaine comes over so we can all walk to Sherilyn's together. She is wearing her new two-piece under denim overalls. I beg her to show me the two-piece, and she finally gives in. It's black, and it fits her just right. Elaine has a bit more (not a lot) than me in the chest department. But even a little makes a big difference. When you're twelve, every bit you've got counts.

Celia braided my hair before she left for Margaret's house, and she even let me borrow her raspberry lip gloss. With Celia helping me, I felt like Cinderella getting ready for her big night on the town. I think I look pretty good.

Elaine and I sit on the porch and wait for Mark to come over. She tells me my hair looks pretty, and I compliment her on her new suit again. I wish I had a two-piece.

We see Mark coming up the walk with a blue towel slung around his neck, and Elaine whispers, "Here comes your one true love."

I kick her and we giggle until Mark makes his way up the driveway. He says, "Hey, Annemarie, hey, Elaine. What are you guys laughing about?"

I tell him none of his business, and the three of us head over to Sherilyn's. The walk over is mostly silent.

Elaine and Mark don't know each other very well. The only thing those two have in common is me, and I get the feeling they're not crazy about each other. Well, it's more than just a feeling. Mark thinks Elaine talks too much, and Elaine thinks Mark is dull. The three of us don't hang out together much anyway. When it's Elaine and me, it's just us, and when it's Mark and me, it's just us too. If truth be told, I like it better that way.

When we get to Sherilyn's house, most of the other kids are already there. Mairi Stevenson and Hadley Smith are sunning on deck chairs. Mairi is wearing a pink two-piece, and Hadley, a yellow polka dot one. (I saw both of those bikinis at the mall, but Mama said she thought a bikini on a twelve-year-old girl was absolutely ridiculous. I think it was because they cost sixty dollars, but Mama would never admit that there was something we couldn't afford. She's a good one for making excuses when it comes to spending money.) Sherilyn's bustling around the food table in a zebra-print tankini. The boys—Kyle, Jack, Tommy, and Hugh Sasser—are in the pool splashing one another.

With the exception of Elaine, us Clementon kids have known each other for most of our lives. We grew up together, learned to ride bikes together, took swimming lessons at the YMCA together. We used to all be friends, at least in the general sense. Somehow the cream of our crop rose to the top, and it's clear we're not all friends anymore. I have a feeling that this will be the last neighborhood back-to-school pool party at Sherilyn's house.

Before Elaine, Sherilyn was my closest girl friend. I still like Sherilyn, but after so many years of knowing each other, the little things started to pile up and bug me. She cares way too much about what Mairi and Hadley think. It's embarrassing. Even when we were little, she was rushing to impress them, rushing to anything them, and she just never measured up. Once Mairi and Hadley and that kind of girl decide you're not good enough, you never will be. You just won't. And the sooner you realize that, the better. Sherilyn has never figured it out. She's so eager to please and imitate that she ends up going overboard.

Like the way her clothes never look right. Mrs. Tallini still picks her school clothes out, and she usually has the right idea, but she takes a good thing too far. If miniskirts are in, Sherilyn will show up in a purple miniskirt with lace trim, plus dangling beads and maybe rhinestones. I do feel slightly guilty for dropping Sherilyn for Elaine, but I didn't really have a choice. Elaine and I are soul sisters. What could I do?

Mark throws his towel on a picnic table and dives into the water. We say hi to the girls, and then Elaine and I spread out our beach towels. We're both reluctant to take off our clothes with everybody there pretending not to look. Elaine unbuckles her overalls, and I throw my T-shirt off in a flash. Why prolong the agony? Elaine's skin is tan and smooth, and I wish I could cover up all my freckles.

Out of the corner of my eye, I see the boys watching us. Elaine and I pretend not to notice, and I know that she's just as aware of the boys as I am. We're doing pretty well until the boys start to snicker, and even then we keep our cool. But then I hear the boys guffawing, and that is pretty hard to ignore.

"I like your bikini, Elaine," Hugh Sasser calls out, and everyone guffaws some more. Hugh is the second cutest boy in our grade, after Kyle Montgomery. He makes red hair and freckles look *good*.

Elaine lifts her head up from the towel, and her hair swings like a silk curtain across her cheek. "I just bet you do, Huey." Her tone is dry, and she rolls her eyes, but I know she is pleased. Elaine knows how to play the game. I look over at Mairi and Hadley, and Hadley looks like she just swallowed a cactus. Hadley's had her eye on Hugh *forever*.

Later Sherilyn's mom brings out a couple of pizzas, and

of course the boys stumble out of the pool and fall onto the pizzas like wild beasts. They're dripping pool water all over the food, and I elbow my way in to get a couple of pieces of pepperoni before they're either soggy or gone. As I inhale my first piece, I overhear Mairi announce that she's on a no-carb diet. Hadley says she wouldn't eat greasy pizza anyway, and Sherilyn looks crestfallen.

Lightly, I say, "Didn't I see you guys eating pizza at the mall last week? Wasn't that you two?" I'm treading extra softly, because challenging Mairi Stevenson in public just isn't done.

"I doubt it," Mairi says coldly. "We don't eat pizza."

"I thought I saw you guys there too," Kyle says. "At Pizza Expresso."

Mairi turns to Kyle and smiles, and it's like I'm not even there anymore. She tilts her chin to one side and coos, "Then why didn't you come over and say hey?" Her thick lashes flutter like twin butterflies. I swear, Mairi Stevenson thinks she's Scarlett O'Hara reincarnated.

I want to say, he didn't come over and say hey because the two of you were too busy stuffing your faces with pizza and he didn't want to interrupt. But I don't dare. I can't afford to burn any bridges with those two. Once they decide to freeze you out, you're done for. I've seen it happen. I'm hanging off the side of a precipice as it is, and the only thing keeping me there is Elaine. I look at her, and she shakes her head slightly.

No one mentions my green one-piece or me until I hear Jack Connelly say, "Her chest is flatter than my back. It's flatter than that diving board." I know he's talking about me, and I want to kill him. I would do it with my bare hands and a smile on my face.

My face is burning and I struggle to keep it devoid of expression, perfectly blank. I have to focus on my rage, or else I will cry. If I cry even one tear because of that cretin, I will never ever forgive myself.

For my sake Elaine is busy pretending she didn't hear a word. She is nattering on about getting a better tan before school starts. "I hardly got tan at all this summer—"

"Jack Connelly is an ass," I hiss.

Elaine whispers, "Just forget it, Annemarie. He's a moron. He has the IQ of a cockroach."

"More like a gnat. A dead, squashed-up gnat."

Full of spite, I jump into the pool. The guys are doing cannonballs off the new diving board Sherylin's dad bought at the beginning of the summer. Wading to the deep end, I bide my time and wait until Jack is just about to jump. At the top of my lungs, I yell, "Choke, Connelly, you big *jack*ass!"

He stumbles and belly flops into the pool. The guys laugh, and I feel somewhat vindicated. When Jack resurfaces, he snarls, "That was so lame, Annemarie. I'd like to see you do better."

"No problem," I say coolly. And it isn't. I know what I can do in the water, and I know I can take down Jack or anybody else any day of the week without breaking a sweat. I've always been a great swimmer, but last summer I went to day camp at the YMCA and I learned all kinds of dives. The swim coach taught me everything, even the flashy stuff. "I might be as flat as a board, but at least I can dive off of one. Ape."

Everyone hoots and hollers, and Jack's face burns red with indignation. He pushes his dark hair out of his eyes. "Let's see it then."

"What's the wager? You better make it worth my while."

"Whatever you want, Wilcox. Name it," Jack says, his confidence returning.

"J, she's pretty good," Mark breaks in. He looks uneasy, and I throw him a dirty look. Where was he ten minutes ago? He should have been sticking up for me back there. He should have been defending my honor. Instead he was busy guffawing with his pals.

"You'd better listen to your buddy, *J*," I taunt. "Your mouth is writin' checks your butt can't cash." I heard Daddy say that on the phone once, on a long-distance business call.

"Just tell me what you want," he snaps.

What do I want? What do I want? I'm frantic, and I say the first thing I think of. "If I win, you carry my books to every class, every day the first week of school." I think I saw that on a *Brady Bunch* rerun on Nick at Nite.

"Carry your books to class?" Jack snorts. "What is this, the 1950s? We have book bags for that, Einstein. Hey, if you wanted to go steady, you should have just said so, Annemarie."

Everyone laughs. My cheeks are on fire. Stupid Nick at Nite! But I manage to say, "Dream on, rat boy. If you're too chicken, you should just say so."

He rolls his eyes. "Fine. And if I win, you carry mine."

"Spit shake." I spit into my hand and hold it out. Jack produces an extra-phlegmy wad of spit, and we shake. I hear Mairi and Hadley squeal, "Ewww."

"The rest of these guys will judge who's the best," Jack says, all business now. "And that'll be me. Don't cry too hard when you lose, Wilcox."

I roll my eyes. We hoist ourselves out of the water and

walk over to the diving board. "Ladies first," Jack says magnanimously. "Oh, wait, I forgot, you're no lady." He snickers.

"Quit stalling and dive," I snap.

Jack struts up the ladder, and he waits until all eyes are on him. "Watch and learn." He somersaults off the board and lands in the water with a big splash. The guys clap. Mairi and Hadley cheer loudly, and Elaine yells, "Booo!"

He swims over to the side, and waits for me to go next. Smirking, he calls out, "Good luck, Wilcox."

"You don't need luck when you've got skills," I say.

I may sound fierce and brave and sure of myself, but my heart is pounding triple time. I've got to nail this dive; I can't let Jack Connelly humiliate me twice. A full gainer would blow his puny somersault out of the water. A full gainer is basically a forward dive where the diver executes a complete backward somersault before hitting the water feetfirst. It's impressive, and it's no easy feat. The hard part is making sure you don't hit the board. It took me most of the summer to get it right, and even then, it's not perfect. Still, me on a bad day is better than Jack Connelly on the best day of his life.

Climbing the ladder slowly, I go through all the pointers Coach Stewart gave me. At the top of the board, I look down and see everyone watching me. I put my hands behind my back to make sure that the hole is still sewn up, and it is, no problems there. Elaine and Sherilyn shout words of encouragement. ("Yeah, Annemarie! Show 'em!") The boys are all standing in the shallow end, and Jack is smirking, but I can see that he is nervous. This makes me feel strong, and I close my eyes and let myself fly.

Magic. That dive was magic. I know I will always remember this moment as golden, my shining moment where I didn't flub anything up, didn't make a fool of myself. It was the stuff of dreams. Under the water I can hear the cheering, and I take my sweet time coming back up. When I do, the applause is deafening. I am a star!

"Annemarie, that was awesome!" from Hugh. A high five from Kyle, who shakes his head and says, "Unbelievable." Even Tommy says, "Where'd you learn to do that?" The girls, even Mairi, ooh and ahh. Beaming, I turn to Mark. But he just says, "Nice job." Last of all, I face Jack, who looks sullen.

"Okay, you win," he says.

I could be gracious about this triumph. I could be generous and let him off easy. But then I wouldn't be me. I crow, "Jacky, was there ever any doubt? You're dealin' with a pro, and you should've known better than to mess with a pro. Go back to the kiddy pool, Jacky. And don't you go tryin' to welch on our little bet like the welcher you are. You lost that bet fair and square. You'd better—"

"I said you win! Geez. You win, okay, Annemarie?"

"And don't forget to meet me at my locker before homeroom."

"We don't need books for homeroom." His ears are pink. I almost feel sorry for him. Almost.

"Who knows? I might want to study before first period. It'll be the first day of junior high and all. But that's not for you to worry about. You just do as you're told, Jacky."

Then Kyle asks me to teach him how to dive, and I would pay big bucks to see that sour look on Mairi's face again. I feel like Mohammed Ali, float like a butterfly, sting like a bee. Winning the mathathon in third grade didn't even come close to how good this feels. I'm glowing from the inside out, like lightning bug guts.

After the party, Mark and I walk home together alone. Elaine's dad picked her up from Sherilyn's house (we planned it out that way), and it's just the two of us. My limbs are sore, and I'm thinking about how good a peanut butter sandwich will taste when Mark says, "Why'd you have to show off like that, Annemarie?"

"WHAT?" I squawk. "What are you talking about?"

"You know you're a good diver. You didn't have to show up Jack. You embarrassed him in front of everybody." Mark's mouth is set in a stubborn line.

"*I* embarrassed *him*? Is that what you think happened today? Because gee, I was remembering how *he* humiliated *me*. And how *you* didn't even stick up for me. Thanks heaps for that, by the way."

He can't even look at me. "What do you mean?"

"Oh, shut up. You know what I mean. You were there. You heard what he said."

At this Mark finally has the decency to look guilty. "Jack was just being a jerk. He didn't mean it."

"You still should have said something."

"What could I have said? He was kidding around. I didn't want to make it into a big deal. Anyway, it's not like you care what anybody thinks."

I do care. I care what people think, and I care that Mark tossed me to the wolves today. I care that he picked his buddies over me, his oldest and most loyal friend. I care a lot.

"You're right, I don't care. I couldn't care two licks what Jack or anybody else has to say about me. But he is a jerk."

"Nah, he's a good guy. He just says dumb stuff sometimes. I'm just sayin' you didn't have to rub his nose in it when he lost."

"And *I'm* just sayin', Jack Connelly got what he deserved today."

Mark shrugs and smiles. "You *were* pretty good."

Everything inside me tingles when he looks at me like that.

We're standing in front of my house, and I throw my towel over my shoulder and start to walk up the driveway. It's been a good day. "See ya, Mark."

"See ya, Annemarie. Oh, hey, you have something on your bathing suit."

"Huh? Where?"

"On your butt." I twist around to see.

Oh God oh God oh God. It's the hole. It's back. How long has it been here? Oh God oh God. Panicked, I tie the towel around my waist and quicken my pace.

"Hey, what was it?" Mark calls after me.

"Mind your own business!"

I storm into the house. The TV is blaring in the family room, and I storm in there too. Mama's lying on the couch. Panting, I run over to the TV and turn it off.

"Shug, you'd better have a good reason for cuttin' into my show."

A good reason? I'll show her a good reason! I rip off my towel and spin around. "It's all your fault, Mama!"

Her lips are pursed, and I can tell she's trying not to laugh. "Darlin', it's not so bad. Maybe no one even saw."

"This is all your fault! You said you could sew!"

"I said I could sew, I never said I was a miracle worker. When you left this house, that hole was sewn up."

"Yeah, well, obviously not very well! Thanks for nothing! Every other girl at that party had a brand-new two-piece, and what did I have? A tore-up, holey one-piece from two summers ago!"

"You're in a right tizzy and you're lookin' for someone to blame, but don't look at me. I did the best I could, Shug." She reaches for the remote control and that's that. Conversation over.

We'll just see about that.

"If Daddy was here, he'd have made sure I had a new suit," I say.

"Well your daddy's not here now, is he?" She turns on the TV and away from me. She always has to have the last word.

"I wish he was here," I mutter. Then I tie the towel around my waist and retreat to my room. After I slam the door nice and hard (but not too hard), I hurl myself onto my bed. It's a good thing Mark was the only one who saw that hole. If Jack had seen it, I never would have heard the end of it. But wait, what if someone else did see it? What if everyone saw it? Was that a smirk I saw on Mairi's face as I was saying good-bye? Did everybody know all along? No, Elaine would have told me. Thank God for Elaine.

I learned two new things today. Lesson number one: The mere threat of junior high is changing everything. Annemarie and Mark as I knew them are a thing of the past. The old Mark would never have let me down today. He'd have fought like a pit bull for me, just like I would have for him. Instead he rolled over on me. Lesson number two: Mama's best just doesn't cut it. It never does; things always end up a big ol' mess.

When Celia comes home, she asks me how the pool party was. I tell her what happened, and she shakes her head. "Mama isn't that great at sewing, Shug. You should have known better. Bring your bathing suit to me." I retrieve it from the wastebasket, and Celia sews the hole up tight. If Celia had been home last night, this never would have happened. I don't know if I'll ever wear my one-piece again, but I feel better knowing that it's back to the way it's supposed to be. Almost.

chapter 8

The first time I ever saw Elaine Kim, she was standing at the bus stop wearing a white parka. She had on a fuzzy white hat, and her hair was sleek and hung straight down her back. Her boots were the kind I wanted, tall with furry white trim. I knew right away we were meant to be friends.

I said, "I like your boots."

She smiled at me and said, "Thanks. I'm Elaine. I just moved here from New York."

Then I said, "New York? Wow. You must really hate Clementon."

"Yeah, pretty much."

I said, "Me too."

She said, "Really? Where are you from?"

"Clementon."

She laughed.

We sat together on the bus, and by the time we got to school, we were like long-lost sisters.

I will always be grateful that I was the first one at the bus stop that day, that it wasn't Hadley Smith or Mairi Stevenson who saw her first. If they had seen her first, they would have recognized her inherent coolness and snatched her away. They would have plucked her off the tree like perfect fruit and made her one of them before she even had a chance to see me.

I've never been one of the supercool girls at school. In sixth grade I was allowed to sit at the cool lunch table, and I was even invited to Mairi's Friday night sleepovers, but only because Mairi's mom always made her invite us girls from the neighborhood. Now that we're gonna be in junior high, I doubt the old rules will apply. Mairi will invite whomever she wants to invite. I know she'll want to invite Elaine. This is because Elaine is special; she is clearly one of them. But she chooses to stay by me.

Some days it feels too good to be true. It's like my days are numbered, like one day soon, she'll realize that I'm a nobody just like Sherylin. One day Elaine will realize that she made a colossal mistake picking me, that she should have chosen Mairi and Hadley after all. But today is not that day.

Today we are buying new school supplies. I look forward to shopping for school supplies all summer. There is something thrilling about fresh notebooks with blank pages and brand-new Magic Markers and clean erasers and fancy fountain pens. Mama lets me buy one new fountain pen per school year because she knows how important it is to me. If you want to write well, you need a fountain pen. You just do.

Mama gives me twenty dollars for school supplies and warns that I'd better bring back the change. I try to battle for twenty-five, but she tells me I'd better hush before she turns that twenty into a ten. I hush up quick. Before she can change her mind, Elaine and I ride our bikes over to the drugstore.

Elaine has her mother's credit card. Money is a funny thing. I never really think about it until I am standing in a store with a crumpled-up twenty and Elaine has a shiny silver credit card and can spend to the high heavens. Not that she would, and not that her parents would let her, but the point is, she could if she wanted to.

I know exactly what I want to buy: one blue fountain pen, two black pens, five binders (one for every class), two packs of college-ruled loose leaf paper, one box of water-color markers, one box of mechanical pencils, and if there's enough money, one bottle of Wite-Out.

Elaine doesn't care about school supplies, and she gets restless as I debate the merits of felt tip pens versus roller ball. As soon as we came in, she threw a pack of ballpoint pens and a couple of notebooks into our cart and proceeded to follow me around with a bored look on her face.

"The roller balls are thirty cents more, but they really do write smoother. And the felt tips tend to run out of ink faster. Elaine, are you listening?"

She's leaning against our cart, and she straightens up. "Huh? Uh, yeah, the felt tip. Get the felt tip."

I roll my eyes and throw the roller balls into the cart.

As we move through the check-out line, Elaine says, "Hey, what do you think of Hugh Sasser? He's pretty cute, right?"

"Yeah, he's pretty cute. Why? You like him?" This is a new development. Elaine has yet to find one boy from Clementon worthy of her affection.

She smiles. "I don't know. Maybe. Depends."

We pay for our school supplies, and I have sixty-seven cents in change.

Tying our bags to our bike handles (Elaine has to take

one of mine), we ride slowly down Grove Street. That's when we see them: boys. Jack and Hugh and Mark horsing around in front of the ticket booth at the Minnie Sax 99-Cent Movie Theater. It's Clementon's historic theater, and it only plays old movies.

"Be cool," Elaine whispers to me. Now the boys have seen us too, and they wave, except for Jack. We take our time riding over.

Mark's wearing a sky blue polo shirt, and his hair is sweaty. He looks terrific, really terrific. "Hey guys," he says. He grins at me and kicks my bike, and I kick his shin.

"What are y'all up to?" Hugh asks, but he only looks at Elaine.

"Back-to-school shopping," she says.

"We're about to watch a movie," Hugh says. "Do you guys wanna come with us?"

At this Jack rolls his eyes and mutters under his breath.

Elaine and I look at each other, pretending to think it over. She shrugs, I shrug. "Yeah, sure, why not?" she says at last.

After we pay for our tickets (Elaine spots me the thirty-two cents), the five of us file into the theater. Now, I know that Elaine wants to sit by Hugh, and I of course want to sit by Mark, and neither of us want to sit next to Jack. It's like walking a tight rope—we have to fix it so that we walk behind or in front of the boy we want to sit next to. Elaine and I figure all this out in one desperately determined look.

Elaine shouldn't have worried, because Hugh makes a beeline for her. I don't have the same kind of luck.

Mark's toward the back, and I stoop down to tie my shoelace to buy time. But while I'm busy tying, he whizzes right by me. I run to catch up, and say, "Hey, have you gone back-to-school shopping with your mom yet?"

"Nah, she's just gonna go pick out the stuff I need." I remember when Mrs. Findley used to take the two of us. We'd sit in the back of the station wagon and compare erasers and pencil cases.

We walk into the theater together, and to my good fortune, I get to sit next to Mark. Elaine is next to Hugh, then Mark, then me, and then Jack, unfortunately. You win some, you lose some.

It's hard to concentrate on a movie when the boy who possesses your heart is sitting mere inches away. I feel hyperaware of all my senses, like I never really knew my own body until this very moment. I wish he would hold my hand. I wish I could hold his hand. But I'm afraid. I'm afraid he can hear my heart beating extra fast when we bump elbows, I'm afraid that what I feel for him shows all over my face. I'm afraid of everything.

Sitting there in the dark, I close my eyes. I imagine that we're on a real date, that it's just the two of us, that—

Jack pokes me on the shoulder, hard. "Wake up, butthead."

I slap his hand away and try to pay attention to the movie.

The movie is over too soon. Walking out of the theater, I feel like a real teenage girl who goes to the movies with boys, and I'm scared but I'm excited, too. As Elaine and I are mounting our bikes, Jack says, "Why do you always wear your hair up, Annemarie?" Before I can answer, he yanks the ponytail holder out of my hair and a few strands come out with it.

I yelp, and my bike falls to the ground with a loud clatter. My cheeks are flaming, and I feel like I have a fever. Stomping on his foot, I yell, "You barbarian! You idiot!" He holds the hairband high above my head. Jack Connelly, the only boy in our class who is taller than me.

My hair is swinging around wildly, and I feel like a cat whose tail has been cut off. "Give it back!" I scream. For some reason I feel like I could cry.

Alongside me, Elaine says, "Give it back, Jack. You're so immature."

He ignores both of us and throws the hairband to Hugh, who grins and throws it to Mark. Mark hesitates, and I think, please don't. Not you too. Then he hands me the hairband. Jack groans and says nastily, "Why don't you give her a kiss good night while you're at it, Findley."

Mark flushes and says, "Why don't you kiss my ass?"

I'm so happy, I feel like my heart will burst right open. Gathering my hair with one hand, I pull it back into a tight ponytail and hop back onto my bike.

Then we go home, us on our bikes and the boys behind us. As we ride, Elaine tells me that my hair looks pretty down, and I should wear it like that more often.

chapter 9

On the last day of summer, the day before school starts, Mark and I ride our bikes until it's dark. Dusk is settling over Clementon, and we just keep riding. Up Sandy Hill Lane and around the block.

I'm afraid of what happens tomorrow. Will he ring my doorbell at 7:30 and walk with me to the bus stop, the way he always does? Will he still share his tangerine with me at lunch?

"Mark?"

"Yeah?"

"Nothin'."

The crickets are hoopin' and hollerin' for all they're worth, and fireflies light up the streets like it's Christmas.

On a night like this it's hard to believe everything won't be this way forever—the two of us on our bikes going round and round. On a night like this, you just want to reach out and freeze time and make it stay like this forever.

"It's past seven. I'd better go in," Mark says as we ride past Sherilyn's house.

"Once more around the block?"

"All right."

We go once more, and then once more after that. The way he's pedaling so slow, I know he doesn't want to say good night any more than I do, 'cause for some reason good night feels too much like good-bye. So neither of us say anything. We just wave and pedal off in different directions.

It's a long time before I fall asleep.

chapter 10

It is the first day of school.

Elaine and I debated on the phone for over two hours last night, going back and forth over what to wear. We recognized the importance of starting our junior high lives on just the right note, with just the right look. Elaine finally settled on a hot pink camisole and her best black miniskirt. I decided to swipe Celia's cotton halter top and wear my new back-to-school jeans.

My hair is down.

We spent a long time deciding whether or not to wear makeup (lip gloss, yes; eye shadow, no), as we didn't want to appear too excited about entering the seventh grade. Nothing is worse than looking like you are trying too hard.

I have always wondered why that is. Trying hard is supposed to be a good thing. It's in my nature to try hard, to strive to be the best. So how do you know when you've crossed that invisible line of what is acceptable and what is uncool?

At 7:25 I sit at the kitchen table and wait for the doorbell to ring, and it never does. At 7:33 I walk to the bus stop alone. When I get there, Elaine is standing with Mairi and Hadley, and Sherilyn is hovering nearby. Her mother has done it again—Sherilyn is wearing a beaded halter top with tight black pants, and her hair is crimped. I can tell she's uncomfortable by the way she keeps pulling the top down so her stomach doesn't show.

Mark stands with the other boys, away from us. He waves, but he doesn't come over. I want to yell, hey, thanks for ditching me this morning, but instead I just wave back.

The morning is warm, and thankfully, it isn't humid. But it's hot enough to make me wish I'd worn shorts instead of my new jeans. Mairi and Hadley are wearing jean skirts, and now I wish that I had worn a skirt too.

Mairi tells Elaine that she likes her outfit. Hadley is quick to agree. Mairi and Hadley and the other cool girls are faintly in awe of Elaine, her New Yorkness and her Koreaness. Elaine is Korean American, and she is the only

Korean American at our school. It gives her a glamorous sort of mystique that no one born in our town could ever possess. She makes being different cool.

Because they like Elaine, Hadley and Mairi say that my shirt is real cute too. I tell them it's Celia's, which impresses them only slightly. Having Celia for an older sister is the only edge I've got, and I try to throw it into conversation whenever I can. I've been doing this for most of my life, so it's lost a bit of its punch.

When the bus finally arrives, we head straight for the back, where we usually sit. Elaine and I exchange worried glances when we realize that the eighth graders sit at the back of the bus, and as seventh graders, we clearly have no business being back there. Mairi and Hadley join right in, as if they know they belong, as if their success is assured. And sure enough, they are giggling and tossing their hair for all it's worth, and the older guys are actually paying them attention.

Elaine and I settle for the middle of the bus instead. Mark sits toward the back with the rest of the cool kids, and the whole ride to school, I keep looking back at him. I watch him laughing and telling jokes. He's forgotten about me already.

When we get to school, Elaine and I have to part ways.

Her locker is on the east wing of school, and mine's on the west. Clementon Junior High is humongous compared to the elementary school. Elaine assured me that it was nothing compared to the schools in New York, but by my standards, it's pretty big. I've been here before, of course. Mama and I used to come for Celia's chorus concerts and her cheerleading competitions. It seemed big then, too.

The halls are jam-packed, and I have to fight my way through the crowds to get to my locker. To my surprise, Jack Connelly, king of the troglodytes, is already leaning against it. He's just had a haircut, and he's wearing a white button-down shirt with the sleeves pushed up. I'd bet anything his mother made him wear that shirt. His arms are crossed and he's scowling, as usual. "Hey," he grunts.

"What do you want?" I snap. I haven't forgotten about the ponytail holder incident.

"I'm here to carry your books, Einstein." Oh, yeah. I'd forgotten all about our bet.

"It's the first day of school. We don't have any books, *Einstein*."

"You're the one who told me you wanted to study during homeroom." He smirks. "You're such a geek. You're the only person I know who'd wanna study during homeroom."

Oh, yeah. I did say that. "You're the one who was gullible enough to believe me. I bet you don't even know what gullible means. Dummy." I shove him to the side, and spin the dial of my combination lock: 12-34-8. I memorized the combination last week. Counterclockwise, clockwise, counterclockwise. And it won't open. I spin it again, slowly, 12-34-8. The stupid locker won't open, and Jack's still standing there smirking. 12-34-8.

He walks away, and calls over his shoulder, "It's clockwise, counterclockwise, clockwise, Einstein."

I hate his guts.

chapter 11

Four minutes just isn't enough time to get from one class to the next. My homeroom is on one side of the school, and my first period math class is on the other. I barely make it on time, but class goes fine. My math teacher's name is Mr. Kenan, and he's cool. He's old—about sixty or so, and he wears his gray hair in a short ponytail. Math is my least favorite subject, but Mr. Kenan's so laid back and easygoing that I think it could be fun.

I get lost on the way to my next class, English with Ms. Gillybush. I run up and down the hallways in a panic, my book bag banging against my shoulders. A nice eighth grader finally points me in the right direction, and when I run into the classroom huffing and puffing, everyone is quiet and sitting in their seats. Ms. Gillybush is going over the roll, and she's already on Zeman, Nestor. Breathing hard, I take a desk near the back and wipe the sweat beads from my nose.

"You must be Annemarie Wilcox."

"Yes, ma'am. Sorry I was late. I got lost and—"

"Just see that it doesn't happen again." She looks at me for so long that I begin to squirm.

"Yes, ma'am."

I keep my head low for the rest of class.

At lunchtime I scan the cafeteria for Elaine. My heart beats very fast as I walk around with my lunch tray, careful not to make eye contact with anyone. We had it so much easier in elementary school with the assigned seats. This is way too much pressure. I breathe a great big sigh of relief when I see Elaine waving me over. She's sitting at a table with Mairi and Hadley.

I sit down across from Elaine. "Hey, guys."

"Hey," they say, looking bored. How does a person look bored on the first day of school, the first day of junior high? I mean, *already*?

Mairi nibbles on a carrot stick. "Have you seen some of the kids from Lincoln Elementary? They're so clueless."

Hadley chimes in. "Totally. I had gym with a few of

them, and those girls didn't even use deodorant. It was, like, sick."

I have to work hard at not rolling my eyes. Elaine and I look at each other from across the table, and I know she's thinking the same thing. I like how we think the same things.

Taking a bite of my ham sandwich, I scan the cafeteria for Mark. He's sitting at a table clear across the room. It looks like a boys-only table—Mark and Kyle and Tommy and Jack, plus some other guys I don't recognize. I keep looking at him, trying to catch his eye, but he doesn't seem to see me.

Then I see Sherilyn, and my stomach lurches. She's in the lunchline, and she keeps looking over at our table. At me. She has that hopeful look in her eye. I do the only thing I can—I look away. Mairi sees her too, and she says, "Oh, God. There's Sherilyn. Don't look at her; she might come over." She glances at me. "No offense, Annemarie. I know she's your friend . . ."

"Not really. I mean, we used to be." I want to add, she used to be your friend too. You ate pizza at her house and swam in her pool every summer since the second grade. You were there just two weeks ago. Instead I say, "I mean, she's kind of immature."

Mairi and Hadley exchange looks, and Mairi says, "She's completely immature. We didn't want to say anything, but the girl is hopeless."

"Totally," Hadley says.

I keep my head down when Sherilyn walks by. She doesn't stop at our table, and some of the tightness in my chest fades away. Yes, she was my friend, but we're in junior high now. Things are different. She was holding me back. I know I could be cool if I didn't have Sherilyn hanging on to me. It's like trying to shimmy up a rope with a moose tied to your ankles. You've just gotta cut that moose loose.

chapter 12

When the bus drops us off, Mark and I walk home together and I'm relieved. On a day like this it's nice to walk home with your oldest friend in the world. I let myself pretend that nothing's changed, that he didn't stand me up this morning and ignore me all day.

"So what'd you think of Ms. Gillybush?" I ask, kicking a rock along the pavement. I want to ask him why he didn't come by this morning, but I don't. That would be like admitting something's wrong, and saying it out loud makes it true.

"She reminds me of your grandma Shirley." We look at each other and laugh. My grandma Shirley is less like a grandma and more like the grumpy old woman all the kids run away from.

After that laugh, everything really does feel normal. We talk about how different junior high is from elementary school, and how our new bus driver seems like a real grouch compared to old Mr. Rubenstein, who drove the elementary school bus. Mr. Rubenstein used to turn a blind eye when we had paper-ball fights, and sometimes he'd bring us Danish butter cookies for no reason at all. By the time we get to my house, things between us feel good again.

So good that I blurt out, "Hey, how come you didn't come by this morning?"

Mark stares at his feet. "Tommy and I walked over together."

"So, what, I couldn't walk with you guys too?"

"You could . . . if you wanted. I didn't figure you'd wanna walk with a bunch of guys." He scuffs his toe along the gravelly street.

"So you figured I'd rather walk alone?"

"Well, yeah."

"You sure it wasn't 'cause you didn't want me around?" My voice is very small, and now it's me who's staring at my feet.

"No . . . but, the guys, you know? They like it to be just us guys sometimes."

"What about you?"

"Aw, you know I don't mind you. It's the guys . . ." His voice trails off. "You wanna ride our bikes over to the creek?"

"Yeah."

We stay at the creek till dark. Just like old times, when we were little kids. And I want to stay here forever, just like this, because I know he won't be picking me up tomorrow morning, or the morning after that.

chapter 13

To my dismay, Jack is standing by my locker again the next morning. He's leaning up against it like he owns it. Shoving him aside, I say, "Look, you can forget about our bet. I'm sick of seeing your face already."

He scowls at me. "You've got a face like the Elephant Man, but you don't hear me complaining. That's because I'm a man of my word."

"You? A man? Ha!" I open my locker and put my social studies books inside. "I'm releasing you from your word, okay?"

Jack shrugs. "Fine by me."

As he walks away, I'm left thinking, *Who's the Elephant Man*? What does this Elephant Man look like? And more important, how does *Jack* know who he is and how do *I* not know? Thoughts like those can drive a girl near crazy. Whoever the Elephant Man is, it doesn't sound good.

In computer class I look up "Elephant Man" and right away, I wish I didn't.

chapter 14

Teachers have always loved me. I am most comfortable when I am the favorite, the pet. I'm good at it. It's what I do. I have never had a teacher dislike me. Until now. Ms. Gillybush more than dislikes me. She hates me.

Ms. Gillybush sits at her desk, tall, straight, and imposing. Her hair is dark but graying, and her eyes are like lead. I could not tell you what color they are; I can only say that they are hard. I am not sure when she decided to hate me, but hate me she does. Her voice is clipped and harsh when she speaks to me, not warm and familiar the way she is with Kara Jane Simpson. ("Kara Jane, why don't you pass out the workbooks, honey.") Kara Jane Simpson and her shiny brown bob with her stupid red headband. It is clear that

Kara Jane is Ms. Gillybush's chosen one, and I, Annemarie Wilcox, am the one she has chosen to hate.

I can hardly bear it. At first I tried to be at my most Annemarie Wilcox, Star Student. I raised my hand for every question, laughed heartily at the few jokes she made, shushed the other kids when they were too loud. All for nothing. Every time I said a word, her eyes narrowed and her lips tightened. I have no idea what I did to offend her, but I sure wish I could undo it.

In class today I raised my hand, and Ms. Gillybush said, "I think we've heard enough from Annemarie for one day. Don't y'all think so, class? Let's let someone else have a chance to answer, hmm, Annemarie?"

The class tittered. My face must have been bloodred. I wasn't just embarrassed, I was *mad*. What gave her the right to treat me like that? What'd I ever do to her?

The whole rest of the day, it's all I can think about. Even now, on the bus ride home, I seethe with anger. "I mean, what gives her the *right*, Elaine?"

"She's a total cow. Don't let her get to you," Elaine advises. I've been talking about Ms. Gillybush since lunchtime, and Elaine is holding up pretty well. By this point, most people would have said just get over it already. Mark wouldn't even have made it through a whole lunch period. Not Elaine, she nods sympathetically and says the sort of things a best friend should say. Things like, "what a witch" and "she's completely insane."

"I tell you, she has it in for me," I gripe, staring out the window.

"Forget her. She's not even worth it."

"Easy for you to say, you've got Mr. Brandt for English. He's cool."

"Yeah, he is cool. Kinda cute, too." She giggles.

"Elaine, that's gross! He's old!"

"He's not old. He's like twenty-eight. My cousin Eugene is twenty-six, and we're totally on the same level. So age really doesn't mean anything. Anyway, it's not like I would do anything about it. I just think he's kinda cute."

"What about Hugh?"

"I think he might like me."

"Duh. Do you like him?"

Elaine shrugs. "I don't know. I'd go out with him, though."

"Hadley Smith'll wet her pants."

The thought leaves a smile on my face the whole ride home.

When we get off the bus, Mark walks with Tommy Malone and they don't wait for me. I walk extra slow so I can pretend that I'm taking my time on purpose, so it doesn't look like I'm trailing after them. Which I am, but it's not like I can help it, seeing as how we're all walking in the same direction.

chapter 15

I'm in my room doing math homework when I hear the car pull into the driveway. I keep working on problem number thirteen until I hear Mama call, "Girls, your daddy's home."

Daddy is the district manager of a sales company. There's an office about thirty miles north of Clementon, but the main office is in Atlanta. He used to have to travel all over, but now that he's district manager, on his way up to becoming regional manager, he's mostly in Atlanta. But sometimes South Carolina, Alabama, Tennessee, and Florida, if he's lucky. I don't know what Daddy sells exactly, but he sells a whole lot of something lately because these days, he's hardly ever home.

When we were little and Daddy came home, it felt like Christmas. He would stand at the foot of the stairwell and bellow, "Where are my girls?" And Celia and I would come running just as fast as we could. We ran so fast the house would shake. And he would take each of us under an arm and throw us around until we were dizzy. Mama would say, "Be careful, Billy!" and we'd just laugh and laugh. Then Daddy'd pretend he'd forgotten to bring us presents, and we'd have to rifle through his suitcase until we found what we were looking for. Perfume for Celia, maybe a yo-yo for me. Hotel soap and a shower cap, if he hadn't had time to buy anything. It's not like that anymore. He still brings presents, but it doesn't really feel like Christmas.

When Daddy is home, we make more of an effort to be "a real family." It's like, Daddy's home, let's pretend like we are the family we should be. Let's go to church on Sunday; let's go to the diner for dessert; let's go to the movies and buy popcorn with extra butter. When we're all together nobody mentions how Daddy's away more than he is home, or how the gaps in between are getting bigger and bigger. A lot of the time, the Wilcox family feels like make-believe.

Celia never wants to go anywhere with us anyhow. She's too busy running around town with her way-cool friends. She'd rather be with them than us, not that I really blame her.

But I do miss her.

I head downstairs to say hello to Daddy, and Celia doesn't

even bother to come out of her room. Mama's cooked a real supper—steak and cauliflower and bread pudding. She's turning the steaks and Daddy's already at the table. As soon as he sees me, Daddy stands up and I launch myself into his arms. My daddy is a handsome man, built strong and lean; his hair is dark blond and his eyes are chocolaty brown. He smells the way he always does, like tobacco and spearmint chewing gum.

"Hey, peanut. How much did you miss me?"

"Tons. What'd you bring me?" Getting excited about Daddy's presents is just for show now. I'm too old to go bananas over a light-up yo-yo or a box of saltwater taffy. But I know he likes giving the presents more than I like receiving them, so I keep up the game.

Daddy laughs. "Wait till after dinner. Where's your sister?"

My whole life that's all my father ever says to me. Where's your sister?

When dinner's ready, Celia finally comes downstairs. She's wearing her nubby yellow bathrobe, and half of her hair is curled. The other half is in a denim scrunchie. If only the football team could see her now.

The four of us sit at the kitchen table, and Daddy asks Celia and me how our first week of school was. Celia says fine. She barely even looks at him when she says it. The corners of Daddy's mouth turn down, and for a moment no one says anything.

Then I say, "Junior high's all right, but my English teacher hates me."

Daddy raises his eyebrows. "You? Impossible. What's her name, Shug?"

"Ms. Gillybush."

He stops cutting his steak. "Anita Gillybush?"

"I guess so. Yeah, that's her. Why? You know her?"

Daddy laughs. "Yeah, your mama and I went to high school with her. Imagine that. Did you know about this, Gracie?"

Mama shakes her head. "No. I don't even remember her."

"Oh, come on. She was the year below us."

"I honestly don't remember, Billy."

"Actually, I'm not surprised." Grinning, Daddy turns to Celia and me. "Girls, your mama was the most popular girl in school. She didn't have time for the little people. Girls like Anita didn't cut the mustard with your mama. Not cool enough, no sir. Heck, I'm lucky she ever looked at me." We've heard him say this a million times over.

Swatting at Daddy with her napkin, Mama says, "Don't believe a word your father says."

She's eating it up, every word. No wonder Ms. Gilly-bush doesn't like me. Once upon a time, Mama must've been snotty to her. Way to go, Mama. Talk about the sins of the father.

Then Daddy asks Celia which boy is in love with her this week. He doesn't ask me of course.

Buttering a biscuit, I say, "Daddy, Celia's a lesbian now. Didn't you know?"

Daddy chokes on his iced tea. "My baby girl a lesbian?"

"Billy, she's pullin' your chain. Celia's no lesbian." Mama shakes her head and laughs.

"Mama's right. I'm not a lesbian. I'm just bi." With that, Celia gets up and puts her plate of half-eaten food in the sink. "Thanks for dinner, Mama. I'm goin' over to Margaret's."

Mama raises her eyebrows. "Your daddy's just come home. Don't you think you should spend some time with the family? We could all go see a movie. Or we could go to the diner for ice cream."

"I have a life, Mama. Daddy doesn't expect me to change my whole life around just 'cause he's in town. Right, Daddy?" Celia smiles her angel smile.

Daddy falls for it every time. "Of course not, princess. You go have fun at Miss Margaret's. Tell her your old man says hey." He winks at her.

Celia gives him a kiss on the cheek and runs off, her one ponytail bouncing.

As soon as she's gone, Daddy turns to Mama and me. "Now what's this about being bi? What's this bi talk?" His forehead creases like a walnut. "Is Margaret her—her girlfriend?"

Mama and I look at each other and laugh our heads off.

Daddy used to tuck me in at night. He'd get the covers nice and tight and say, "Snug as a bug in a rug?" and then he'd hug me, kiss me on each cheek. It was nice. Now he doesn't come too close.

I'm reading a book in bed, and he stands in the doorway. "Is that your homework, Shug?"

"Nah, it's just for fun." I put the book down, hoping he'll come in and ask me what it's all about, the way he used to. "What's this one all about," he'd say, thumbing through the pages. I'd screech, "Give it back, you'll lose my page!" But I didn't really mind. I liked telling him about my books. My daddy's not much of a reader.

Daddy just nods. "Don't stay up too late," he says, closing the door.

I never felt as safe as I did when he would tuck me in at night.

chapter 16

The first night is always good. There's good food and good talk; they make each other laugh. They smile at each other, secret little smiles over the dinner table. They've forgotten grievances for the time being; they're just enjoying each other's company. On the first night, I can relax. Daddy's remembering all over again how pretty Mama is, how clever. And the only time Mama really seems alive is when he's looking at her. She tells fantastical stories about whatever happened at the nursing home while Daddy was gone. My mama knows how to tell a good story. Old Mr. Schuman and his trumpet or Mrs. Kirkpatrick and her sparkly red dress. I've heard all her stories before, but I still lean forward and listen like it's the first time. When I go to bed, I'm full on steak and stories.

And the second night's okay. I can count on the second night being okay.

It's the third night that's the problem.

They sit at opposite sides of the den—Mama on the far end of the couch, reading a book with a glass of red wine, Daddy in his easy chair watching TV with a beer. Each pretending the other doesn't exist. Maybe not even so much pretending. So what's the point of sitting in the same room? It's not to be near each other, I know that much. At no point does Mama look up from her book and wiggle her nose at Daddy, and he certainly doesn't take his eyes off the TV screen to wink at Mama.

And me, I'm sitting at my perch, the dining room table, with my homework all laid out in front of me. If I'm here, then nothing bad can happen. That's what I tell myself, anyway. I sort of believe it too.

Moments like these, when the air is thick and the night feels like forever, I wish I was Celia. Not because she's prettier or more popular, but because she's older. She's old enough to have places to go to. There's one place in particular—college. I imagine she whispers it to herself at night, when no one else can hear. *College.* College, the

Promised Land, with no Mama and no Daddy. And no me.

When Celia leaves, I'll be all alone. With Mama and sometimes Daddy. Celia's hardly here as it is, but just knowing she's nearby makes me feel safer.

Still, the big problem isn't Celia leaving. She's nearly gone already. It's me. I've got five more years at home, but what happens when I leave home too? When I'm gone, who will keep watch? Mama and Daddy need me here. When Daddy's gone, it's my job to take care of Mama, and when he's here, it's still my job.

She's different when he's home. We all are. When Daddy's home, Celia and I don't walk around in our underwear. Mama wears lipstick, and she stays home at night. And poor Meeks isn't allowed on the couch.

It's strange to come home from school and see Daddy mowing the lawn or cleaning out the garage. It's like he's this extra piece of a puzzle that doesn't fit, and you have to keep moving the pieces around to readjust your whole way of thinking. So you end up changing the whole puzzle around, just so he'll fit. We all do it in our own ways.

By the end of the week, Daddy's itching to leave, and we're ready for him to go.

chapter 17

When I get home from school, Celia and Mama are having one of their blowout fights. I can hear Celia yelling before I even open the front door. It turns out that Mama forgot to deposit Daddy's paycheck, and the check for Celia's SAT prep course bounced.

Celia's pacing back and forth in the kitchen, and Mama's sitting at the table holding a wet washcloth to her forehead. I stand in the doorway, ready to jump in, smooth things over.

"It's not the end of the world," Mama says. "You still have plenty of time."

Celia shakes her head so furiously her dangly crystal earrings swing back and forth. I love those earrings. If Celia ever died, God forbid, they are what I'd want. To remember her by, and all. "It's gonna be all your fault when I go to Lincoln Community College, Mama," she rages. "You talk a big talk about Annemarie and me leaving this town, but deep down I think you wanna keep us here. You want us to be miserable just like you."

"Oh, Celia. Always the drama queen, aren't you, darlin'? I'm really gettin' sick of you and your lady-of-the-manor routine." Mama sips from her tall glass of iced tea. I hope it's just sweet tea, but I have a feeling it's Long Island.

"I hate you," Celia says quietly. I know she means it.

"Of course you do. You're sixteen."

Celia runs upstairs, and I follow her. I creep into her room, where she's sitting on the bed, staring out the window. "Get out," she says. She doesn't even look at me.

Sitting down next to her, I say, "Aw, come on, Celia. You can still take the class next month, right?" I pat her on the shoulder awkwardly.

Celia acts like she doesn't hear me. "When I get out of here, I'm never coming back." I'm not sure if she's talking to me or herself, and I'm a little scared.

"You don't mean that. You're just mad right now."

"You're such a little baby. You don't understand anything. Our family sucks. I'm never coming back."

I recoil. "How can you say that? You're my sister."

She finally looks at me then, and her green eyes are sad. "You've gotta grow up, Shug. You've gotta see people for who they are. I can't keep on taking care of you forever."

"Taking care of me?" I repeat. "You're never even home. *I'm* the one taking care of things around here."

"I'm so sick of caring about what happens. Nothing ever changes." She stares out the window some more, then says, "Just get out, Annemarie."

"Fine." I stalk out of her room and go to mine.

I'm almost done with my homework when Mama calls us down for supper. She's gone to the grocery store and gotten pork chops and applesauce and baked potatoes with sour cream. I'm surprised that she's cooked, but I know why. She cooks when she knows she's done wrong by us, when she wants to make amends without actually saying sorry. Which she never does—say sorry, I mean.

I know a good thing when I see it. A real dinner is plenty apology enough for me. I lean close to the plate and breathe in the smell of sizzling pork and cinnamon apples.

"Where's your sister?" Mama's only got one pork chop on her plate and a dab of apple sauce. I'll know that I'll probably be finishing her leftovers because Mama never really eats when she's been drinking.

Dipping a pork chop in apple sauce, I say, "She went over to Margaret's house. Not that I blame her."

"Don't you start on me too."

"I'm just sayin'. The SATs are a pretty big deal. I can see why she's mad. Couldn't you have been more careful, Mama? I mean, you shoulda known how much was in the checking account. And then you didn't even say sorry . . ." She glares at me, and I stuff half a pork chop in my mouth to keep from saying anything else.

"I do the best I can by you girls." Sighing heavily, Mama cuts into her pork chop and takes a small bite. She doesn't say anything more, and in this light, the circles under her eyes look dark and bleak. She looks old.

I feel guilty for harping on her, but I'm still able to finish the rest of my supper with gusto. My mother hardly ever cooks, so when she does, it feels like a special occasion. Burping, I reach for one of Celia's pork chops, but quick as lightning, Mama snatches the plate away.

"I'm saving this for your sister, for when she gets back. She might want a snack. You eat the rest of mine; I'm not hungry." She gets up from the table and covers Celia's plate with plastic wrap.

"You sure?" I'm already reaching for her pork chop.

"Yes, greedy. And there's mint chocolate chip ice cream

in the freezer." Mint chocolate chip is Celia's favorite. It tastes like toothpaste to me, but hey, I'll eat it. Ice cream is ice cream. Mama puts the plate in the refrigerator and says she needs to take a nap. She leaves me alone in the kitchen, and I polish off the rest of the pork chop, taking care to swirl it around in her little mound of apple sauce.

When she makes the effort, she's not a bad cook. Not great, not like Mrs. Findley, but not bad.

Celia comes back home when I'm doing the dishes. She throws her pink purse on the kitchen table. "Is she around?"

"No, she's asleep. We saved you some dinner, though. It's in the fridge."

"I ate at Margaret's."

"But she made pork chops . . ." My voice trails off when I see Celia's hard face. I turn back to the dishes and scrub the greasy skillet a little harder. "There's ice cream, too."

Grudgingly, she says, "What kind?"

"You know what kind."

Celia purses her lips and walks over to the freezer. She pulls out the carton and sits down at the table.

Wiping my soapy hands on my jeans, I give her a big spoon and sit down next to her. "She feels really bad, you know." I pry the lid off the frosty carton and slide it over to Celia.

She sniffs. "I don't want to talk about her."

"Fine, fine."

Celia scoops herself a big spoonful of ice cream and nibbles on it. "Tell me what's goin' on with you and Kyle."

"Huh? Me and Kyle?"

Celia rolls her eyes. "Yeah . . . the boy who taught you how to love?"

Oh, yeah. "Um, I don't know. I hardly ever see him. Junior high's pretty different."

"What do you mean, different?" She licks her spoon like a cat.

I take a big bite of mint chocolate chip. "Everybody's actin' different, is all. Mark especially. He acts like he's forgotten all about us being best friends. All he cares about is hanging out with the guys. I went over there the other day, and he was leaving to go play basketball, and then he didn't even invite me."

"So?"

"So he always invites me! And it's more than just that. At school he barely even looks at me."

"Well, boys are like that, Shug."

"I know," I say. "Wait, what do you mean? What are they like?"

"They take you for granted sometimes. They care more

about looking cool than being your friend. But I promise you, Mark hasn't forgotten you. How could he? You're like brother and sister."

Frowning, I say, "Well, I wouldn't say brother and sister exactly."

"Pretty close to it. Y'all were raised up together. Shug, just give him time to get used to junior high. He'll figure out who his real friends are sooner or later."

Celia inherited Mama's talent for makin' you forget and she doesn't even need ice cream. I forgive her for what she said earlier. No matter what she says, I know she'll always come back home.

chapter 18

I asked Mark if he wanted to come over and quiz each other on the fifty states and capitals, and when he asked me if anyone was going to be home, I said yes. I told him Celia would probably be there, and I knew it was wrong even as I was saying it. I felt cheap and terrible, and when he said okay, I still felt cheap and terrible but happy, too.

Sitting at the kitchen table, drinking Cokes and eating peanuts, I'm filled with such gladness for this moment. To be here with Mark, just like this. Just us two, just like before.

He tosses a peanut my way, and I catch it with my mouth. This is our trick; we are good at it. He throws, and I catch.

And then Celia comes home and ruins everything.

"What are you doing home?" I blurt out. Guiltily I glance at Mark, but he's too entranced to even notice.

Celia's cheeks are pink, and her hair is falling out of her ponytail in tiny damp ringlets. She puts her book bag on the kitchen table and gives me a funny look. "Hello to you too, Shug. Practice finished early today." Then she smiles at Mark, and she's like the sun, shining down on a grateful little daisy. He blushes with pleasure. "Hey there. Where've you been, Mark? I haven't seen you around here in forever."

I'm boiling as he hems and haws and stutters that uh, he's been, uh, around. I can't help but glare at them both.

Then Celia sits down with us and goes on about her stupid cheerleading practice. Mark's eyes are wide and he's nodding at everything she says, like he even knows what a herkie is. He can't take his eyes off her in that baby blue angora sweater. Yeah, I know what he can't take his eyes off of.

It's like I've stopped existing. I'm not even in the room anymore. I'm mad at him, and I'm mad at her, too, and it's not even her fault. She can't help the way she looks in baby blue or the way her hair curls around her ears, any more than I can help the way I look. But that doesn't stop me from being mad at her.

When Celia takes her Coke upstairs, I turn on Mark. "You just made *such* a fool of yourself." I'm so angry I'm practically biting each word out.

"What are you talking about?" he says uncomfortably. He stuffs a handful of peanuts into his mouth and does not look in my direction.

"You were slobbering all over her. You need to get a grip on reality. Celia's in *high school*. You think she would ever go for a little kid like you?"

"You're crazy, you know that?" Mark gets up and starts shoving his notebooks into his book bag. "I'm going home."

"Fine, go home. But don't blame me when you flunk the quiz!" I yell.

I hope he flunks the quiz.

chapter 19

Ms. Gillybush hands back our essays, and when I see my grade, I nearly choke. I got a B? I have never gotten a B in English in my entire life. English is what I'm supposed to be good at.

She stands in front of her desk and says, "With the exception of a few students, I'm disappointed in the caliber of these essays. Frankly I expected a higher level of quality from honors students." Ms. Gillybush stares at us stonily, and Kara Jane preens and twists around in her seat. I bet *she* got an A.

"But as mediocre as your essays were, they weren't nearly as appalling as my non-honors-student essays. Therefore I am offering an incentive program. You will have the option of earning extra credit by tutoring strug-gling students outside of school hours. Should I see an improvement in your tutee's work, I will award you extra credit. After class you can sign up and after school today there will be a meeting in my classroom. If you're inter-ested, I expect to see you there."

After class a group of us huddle around Ms. Gillybush's desk. She passes around a clipboard listing the names of kids who need help, and we sign our initials next to the person we want to tutor. When the clipboard finally gets to me, every name is taken but one. Jack Connelly. Uh-uh. No way. I scan the rest of the list, and I see that Martin Lum has picked Mark. Martin and I were in Ms. Dunbar's sixth-grade class together last year.

Martin is short with thin brown hair, and he wears thick glasses that slip down his nose. Probably 'cause his nose is greasy. He's hoisting his book bag on his shoulders when I say, "Martin, you wanna trade with me?"

He eyes me suspiciously. "Why, who do you have?"

"Jack Connelly."

Shaking his head, he says, "Uh-uh. No way. That guy used to give me wedgies. No way am I helping him. Sorry, Annemarie."

"Aw, come on—"

Ms. Gillybush breaks in crisply. "Annemarie Wilcox, this isn't a popularity contest. You can either be a part of this program or not, but I won't have you complaining over who you get."

"Yes, ma'am." Slowly, I write my initials next to Jack's name, and then put the clipboard in Ms. Gillybush's outstretched hand. I feel like Faustus, signing my life away to the devil himself.

Celia was supposed to read the play *The Tragical History of Doctor Faustus* for English Literature last year, but she ended up watching the movie instead. We watched it together. I really don't think someone who watches high-school-level movies should be getting a B in English. Anyway, in the movie, this guy Faustus sells his soul to the devil in exchange for magical powers. The big moment is when he signs the contract in his own blood. That's why people say things like "Faustian bargain" or "Faustian moment." I'm having a real Faustian moment right now (minus the blood part). I just hope I don't live to regret it the way Faustus did.

The rest of the day moves by way too fast. When I walk into Ms. Gillybush's room that afternoon, everybody else has already paired off. Jack's sitting alone, and as soon as he sees me, he groans. "Aw, man. Not you."

I slam my book bag on the floor and sit down across from him. "Trust me, I don't wanna be doing this either. Not with you, that's for sure."

"Then why are you?" he says nastily.

"Because I got a B on my essay, and I need the extra credit, not that it's any of your business," I snap.

"Oh, poor widdle Annemarie, she got a B. Big deal. Your life is so hard."

"Just shut up. I'm the one who's helping you, you ingrate."

"And I'm *so* grateful."

We snipe back and forth until Ms. Gillybush claps her hands. "Get to work, people. Decide when and where you're going to meet."

We glare at each other, and I finally say, "So when do you wanna have our first tutoring session?"

"How about never?"

"Fine by me, but I'm not the one who's gonna have to go to summer school for failing English."

That shuts him up quick. "I can't after school. I've got baseball practice."

"Then when? I'm not giving up my lunch period."

"Fine. I'll come by your house after dinner then," he says, like he's doing me some big favor when *I'm* the one doing the favor.

"Not my house. I'll come to yours."

He shrugs. "Whatever. Tuesday night?"

"Yeah, okay."

If I'm lucky, Tuesday night will never come.

chapter 20

In all the years I've known Jack, I've never been inside his house. I guess it's no surprise, seeing as how we hate each other and all. After supper I ride my bike over very slowly.

Jack's house is the small blue one-story with light blue shutters on the corner of Two Waterfalls Street. I ring the doorbell, and I realize my hands are sweaty. I've been dreading this moment all day.

I hear feet running to the door, and a little girl opens it. She looks about four years old. She's wearing yellow overalls and her hair is tied in two braids. There's ketchup on her chin. She's Clarice, Jack's little sister. "Are you my friend?" she asks. Her dark eyes are enormous.

I smile at her. "I'm Annemarie. You've met me before, Clarice. At the pool sometimes, remember?"

She nods. "Yeah . . . at the pool." She's opening the door wider when Jack walks up behind her, saying, "Clary, who is it? You know you're not supposed to open the door to strangers. . . . Oh, it's you."

We stare at each other for a minute. Then Clarice takes my hand and pulls me inside the house. "She's not a stranger; she's my friend," she tells Jack. She sticks her tongue out at him.

"Yeah," I say. I stick my tongue out too.

He rolls his eyes and lets Clarice lead me through the house. "This is the kitchen, this is the potty room, and this is the TV room." The house is dim, and there are toys strewn all over the place, in every room.

We end up in the TV room, where Clarice tells me to sit on the couch. I obey, and she plops down in my lap and plays with my hair. The couch is threadbare, and there are dark stains all over the cushions. I think I smell peanut butter on the cushion I'm sitting on.

Clarice says, "Annie Mary, your hair is pretty."

Jack snorts loudly. "Ha ha. It's about as pretty as a donkey's tail."

"You little—"

He interrupts me before I can say what I'm thinking, which is probably a good thing, because you shouldn't cuss in front of kids. "Clary, you gotta leave us alone now. Annie Mary and I need to get some work done."

Clarice shakes her head, and her braids swing back and forth. "Uh-uh. Annie Mary's my friend. She's here to see me. Right?"

"Uhh . . . It's true that I'm your friend, but Jack and I have to do our homework first. Maybe we can play later?" I glance at Jack, and he looks disgusted. He probably doesn't want me to stay a second longer that I have to.

"Nah. Now. I wanna play now."

Jack walks over to us and picks Clarice up. "Nooo," she whines.

She tries to wriggle out of his arms, but he has a tight grip on her. Jack whispers something in Clarice's ear and carries her out of the room. He returns a minute later without Clarice. "We can work at the kitchen table, I guess," he says. I shrug and follow him into the kitchen. There are two dirty plates on the table, and Jack puts them in the sink. The sink is piled up pretty high already. Some of the plates look crusty; I wonder how long they've been there and also if Jack knows that you're supposed to let plates soak in hot water and soap so they won't get all crusty like this.

We sit down across from each other.

"So what next?" He looks at me challengingly, but I'm ready for him.

"Go get your essay. We'll start there."

"Whatever you say." His book bag is on the kitchen table, and he digs around inside until he finds it. He hands me a crumpled piece of paper with a D- written across the top. D-, wow. So he really is dumb. How did he ever pass the sixth grade?

Smirking, I say, "Nice one, Einstein. No wonder you need a tutor."

Jack bristles and snatches the paper away. "I don't need you giving me a hard time, Wilcox. If you're gonna start up on me, then you can just get out."

"Okay, okay. I was just kidding. Geez. Look who's Mr. Sensitivo all of a sudden. He can dish it out but he can't take it." I can't stop smiling.

Glowering at me, he says, "Are you gonna help me or not?"

"Fine, fine." I skim over the essay, and it's in pretty bad shape. It's a mess of misspelled words, jumbled-up thoughts, and poor subject-verb agreement. I can see that I have my work cut out for me with this one.

• • •

We're still working when Jack's mom gets home. Like Mama, Mrs. Connelly doesn't come out for neighborhood cookouts. She works a lot, and ever since she and Jack's dad split up, she's stopped bothering with being social.

Mrs. Connelly has dark hair like Jack, and pretty eyes, but there are deep wrinkles that border the skin around the edges. She's wearing her waitress uniform, and she smells like restaurant food and smoke. She has a run in her stocking.

She puts half of a chocolate pie on the table. There's a mound of whipped cream in the middle, and chocolate shavings sprinkled on top.

"Hey there," she says. "Who's your friend, Jacky?" Her bangs look damp, and she runs her hand through them, fixing them till they fall right.

"Mom, this is Annemarie," Jack mumbles. He barely looks up. "We're studying for English."

"Hi, Mrs. Connelly," I say.

"Call me Trish, honey. Mrs. Connelly is my mother-in-law, and trust me, you don't want to meet *her* in a dark alley." She laughs. "Right, Jacky?"

He mutters, "She's your *ex*-mother-in-law."

"Right, right." To me, she says, "So you're brave enough to help out my boy, huh?"

"Yes, ma'am, I guess so," I say.

She sits down next to Jack and smoothes his hair over to one side. He jerks away from her. "Would you kids like some pie?"

I'd love some pie, but before I can say so, Jack says, "No, Annemarie has to get home."

Trish looks at me then, her eyes narrowing. "Annemarie, you look familiar. Wait a minute, you're Grace and Billy's little girl, aren't you?"

"Yes, ma'am."

"Well, you look just like her." She lights a cigarette and inhales deeply.

I hate it when people say I look like Mama. Mostly because it isn't true. I look nothing like her.

Trish tugs at her collar and smiles at me tiredly. I can't stop staring at those wrinkles around the corners of her eyes. She has such nice eyes too. Maybe if she used Mama's kind of eye cream . . .

"If I'd have known we were having company, I'd have cleaned up the house a bit," she says. "You sure you can't stay for some pie?"

For a second, I consider saying yes. The pie looks good, and Jack looks like he's in serious pain, which is a good thing. Anything to prolong his agony. But, I know what it feels like to be embarrassed by your mother, and I wouldn't wish it on anyone. Not even Jack. "No, ma'am, I'd better get going." She protests, but I pack up my things quick as I can, and I hurry on home.

It's a sad thing to feel sorry for an adult. There's something wrong about it; you're not supposed to feel sorry for the people who take care of you. They're supposed to be older and wiser. But Jack's mom just looks tired.

chapter 21

My sister has cool friends. I guess it makes sense for her to have cool friends, because Celia herself is cool. My favorite friend is her best friend Margaret. Margaret has long reddish blond hair with a side part, and she has very slim wrists. She wears a gold heart-link bracelet every day, on her right wrist. I think her father must have given it to her. He died years ago, a heart attack while he was mowing the front lawn. Maybe that's why Margaret has such slim wrists, so she can still wear the bracelet her father gave her all those years ago.

The other day, Margaret was over and they stayed up in Celia's room forever, the way they always do. As soon as she and Celia get home from school, they rush upstairs and turn the music on and I can't hear a thing. I even turned the TV down low.

They came down after a few hours though, and they just took over the whole TV room. Celia shoved my legs over and took two whole couch cushions for herself, and Margaret grabbed the remote control like she owned it. I didn't really mind, though, because I like when Margaret and Celia hang out with me. Well, they weren't really hanging out with me, but they were in the same room as me, and that's pretty much the same thing.

We were watching a music video when Margaret said, "Hey Annemarie, you got a boyfriend yet or what?"

I said no, and Celia said, "Yeah right. Who's gonna go out with *her*?" But she smiled when she said it, so I wasn't mad.

And then Margaret winked at me and she said, "Cel's just jealous, Annemarie, 'cause you're way prettier than she was when she was your age."

Celia threw a pillow at her, and we all laughed, but inside, I was dancing. I was spinning all around on my tippy-toes with my arms high in the sky, and all because Margaret said I was pretty. I know it isn't true; I remember what Celia looked like when she was twelve, and it's the same as she looks now. Beautiful. But I don't care, because just for a minute, I believed it.

Sometimes I wish Margaret was my sister.

chapter 22

Fall is my favorite time of the year. The air smells so good and clean. I like the falling leaves, the apple cider, but I love Halloween most of all. There's a hush in the air on Halloween night; it's practically religious. Waiting for night to finally appear. Rushing out into the neighborhood like a warrior. Feeling the weight of your pillowcase grow heavier and heavier with all things chocolaty, tart, and delicious. That sweet anticipation after you ring the doorbell—will you be lucky enough to get two pieces of candy if you smile and say "ma'am"? And then returning home with your bounty. Emptying your pillowcase and counting each piece so very carefully. And ah, November 1—Trading Day. What can be more thrilling than ripping somebody off by trading two lousy lollipops for a fun-size Nunko bar? Yes, the candy is exciting, but the costumes, those are the very best part. I will never get tired of dressing up. It's fun to pretend to be someone else for just one day.

Celia thinks I'm too old to get dressed up and go trick-or-treating, and maybe I am. Maybe she's right, maybe it is time to put away my pillowcase and give up chasing my old candy dreams. But I don't want to. I said, "If I'm too old for dressing up, then what about all those adults that go to masquerade balls and costume parties? Are they too old too?"

Anyway, Celia won't let Elaine and me go to Margaret's Halloween party (where nobody's gonna be dressing up, which sounds pointless to me), so what else are we gonna do? We're twelve, so I think we can fly under the radar and trick-or-treat this one last time, just for kicks. That's the case I made to Elaine, anyway. I said we'll just go out for an hour or so, no one will even see us and we'll get free candy. She caved, mostly because she never really got to go trick-or-treating in New York 'cause her parents thought it was too dangerous. She had to go to her school's autumn fest, and that's not how you celebrate Halloween. You've gotta be out on the streets.

Daddy's home again. He and Mama are going to a

Halloween party at the Honeycutts'. Jim Honeycutt works with Daddy, and he was transferred over to the Clementon offices not too long ago. The Honeycutts just moved here, and already they're throwing parties. I can't remember the last time Mama and Daddy had anybody over to the house. Mama grumbled about having to go to a Halloween party, but she sure spent some time thinking about her costume.

Daddy's wearing his tux. He says he is Double-Oh-Seven. I said, what's Double-Oh-Seven, and he laughed. "Bond, James Bond," he said. "Don't you know who James Bond is?"

I said, "Yeah. I'm not stupid. I just didn't know the Double-Oh-Seven part. What does that mean, anyway?"

Daddy changed the subject quick. I don't think he knows what it means either.

It took me most of September to think up my costume. I'm a mad scientist. I got Celia to crimp my hair and tease it out, and I'm wearing a lab coat from science class.

"You look cute, Shug," Daddy reaches out to ruffle my hair, and I twist away before he can mess it up. "Where's your sister?"

"Margaret Tolliver's throwing a Halloween party, and Celia won't even let me go. She never takes me anywhere.

So me and Elaine are gonna go trick-or-treating, just for kicks." He isn't even listening to me anymore; he's looking over my shoulder.

It's Mama walking down the stairwell in her Helen of Troy costume. Her hair is piled high on her head, and she is wearing a white silk dress with an empire waist and folds and folds of silk. Daddy looks at her like she's the only person in the room, in the world. This makes me feel safe. I know there won't be any fighting tonight, just loving. I won't have to put my headphones on to drown out their yelling. I won't hear a thing. I'll just sleep.

That's how it is with my parents. It's all or nothing. They fight like tomcats, and then they make up for it later.

"You're beautiful," Daddy says, like it's a fact. And it is. She is. He reaches out and touches her cheek, and she smiles a secret smile meant only for him.

All of a sudden my father remembers that I am there too, and he says, "Isn't your mama beautiful, Shug? Isn't she somethin'?"

She's somethin' all right. I don't say anything, and it doesn't matter, because they won't hear me anyway. Daddy helps Mama with her coat, and he tells me to be good and have fun.

To be good and have fun. Can you be good and have fun all at the same time? Is that even possible?

I wonder.

As soon as it starts to get dark, I head over to Elaine's. Mrs. Kim makes a big fuss over my costume and takes about a million pictures of the two of us. Elaine is dressed up as Daisy from *The Great Gatsby*. We got the idea when we were flipping through channels one afternoon, and *The Great Gatsby* was on the old movie network. Elaine had never heard of it, but I'd read it last summer because it was on Celia's reading list.

Mrs. Kim spent two weeks sewing Elaine's costume, and it shows. Elaine's dress is a silky periwinkle blue, and she's tied a lace sash just below her hips. She's wearing a shiny blond wig cut in a bob, and a pearl and feather headpiece. And dark red lipstick. She's not usually allowed to wear makeup, but her mother let her just this once because it was a special occasion.

We run into the boys on Thurston Street. When I see the way the boys look at Elaine, my stomach turns. Mark stares at her like he's never seen a girl before. Even Jack looks at her, and he doesn't look at any girl. I feel silly in my mad scientist costume, and to think I'd been so proud of it just a few minutes before. I'd thought it was such a clever idea, and now it feels all wrong. I wish I'd picked something glamorous instead of something babyish. I'm the one with the blond hair; *I* should have been Daisy instead of a stupid mad scientist. It was *my* idea.

Hugh whistles. "Who are you?" he says admiringly. He isn't looking at me, of course.

"Duh, I'm Daisy from *The Great Gatsby.*"

"What's that?" Hugh says.

"It's a book; it's famous." She bats her fake eyelashes at him and says, "The schools down South really are deficient. Can you even read, Huey?"

I bristle. Elaine has a lot of nerve talking about the South like that. She didn't even know who Daisy was until I told her.

Whooping, Hugh grabs the headpiece from her head and takes off running down the street. Elaine laughs and chases after him, tottering in her heels.

The rest of us stand around awkwardly. It's cold outside, and at least my lab coat is keeping me warm. Well, warmer than Elaine in her skimpy little dress, anyway.

Jack pokes my hair, and I slap his hand away. Laughing, he says, "Your costume's not half bad, Einstein."

I flush. I hadn't even thought of that. I hadn't gotten the idea from him, had I? And Einstein wasn't really a scientist, he was more of a mathematician. Wasn't he? He did have that wild hair, though. . . .

chapter 23

My whole life I wanted to eat at Mark's house for Thanksgiving dinner. I almost got my wish a few years back when
Daddy couldn't come home because of work, and Mama
got so drunk she forgot to put the turkey in the oven. I was
looking forward to eating that turkey all day, and then dinnertime came, and I asked Mama, when do we get to eat?
She said, "Damnation!" And that turkey was still frozen
solid in the refrigerator. I threw a fit—all I ever wanted was
that turkey! Turkey for dinner and turkey sandwiches all
week. I said that I was going to the Findleys' for dinner,
and Mama said absolutely not. While I was crying upstairs,
she went to Kentucky Fried Chicken and bought a twenty-
piece bucket. She got a family-size portion of mashed pota-

toes, extra biscuits, and two corn on the cobs just for me. Mama got that part right at least.

Thanksgiving is a big deal at Mark's house. They even hang a turkey flag on the front porch. Mrs. Findley starts cooking three days in advance. Food prep, she calls it, so there's less to do on the big day. I'd help her by doing little things—chopping onions and rolling out piecrust, stuff like that. She always makes exactly the same dishes, and I know it all by heart. Turkey with giblet gravy, fresh-baked yeast rolls, cranberry sauce from scratch, sweet corn pudding, green bean casserole, real mashed potatoes, whipped sweet potatoes with baby marshmallows, oyster stuffing (homemade, not box), pumpkin pie and pecan pie (homemade, not store bought). Mark's grandparents come all the way from Detroit, and the men work on Mr. Findley's antique train set. I'm not sure what the women do. I guess they cook. I never bothered to ask.

This year we're having guests too. Well, we are now, anyway. Daddy called last Monday and said that he'd invited the Honeycutts over for Thanksgiving dinner. You can just bet that Mama wasn't too happy about that one. She lit into him good. She called Daddy a selfish, good-for-nothing louse of a husband. She also said that the last time she saw him, he'd put on some weight, and maybe he'd be better off skipping Thanksgiving dinner altogether. I'm surprised the whole neighborhood didn't hear some of the names she was calling him.

Mama cleans the house all week. She even vacuums. She assigns Celia and me jobs too. I cleaned the downstairs bathroom, made sure the guest towels were out, and Celia dusted the family room. She's also in charge of the biscuits and stuffing. I'm in charge of the yams and the pumpkin pie. That leaves the collard greens, mashed potatoes, and turkey for Mama. Daddy doesn't get any jobs because he comes home the night before Thanksgiving, so late that I'm already in bed.

I hear the car pull in the driveway. There was a time when I'd run downstairs so I could be the first to see him, but now I just stay in bed, straining to hear Mama and him talk. I can't hear anything, though.

Thanksgiving night the Honeycutts arrive right on time. There's Jim Honeycutt, who Daddy works with, Lana Honeycutt, who doesn't work at all, and Micah Honeycutt, who goes to Clementon High with Celia—not that they hang around the same crowd. Micah has a fierce case of acne and an attitude to match. He and Celia's kind don't really mix. They mutter hey to each other, and that's pretty much it.

I figure it's up to me to be a good hostess so I try to talk to Micah, but he looks at me like I am a bug. We all sit around the den, smiling at one another. Except for Micah, who just scowls.

Mr. Honeycutt is wearing a navy pinstriped suit, and Mrs. Honeycutt has on a pink cashmere sweater set, and a gold charm bracelet that jangles. Her hair is auburn, and it's pulled up in a French twist. It looks hard and stiff. I wonder if she did it herself or if she had it done.

Mama's wearing a black satiny blouse and black cigarette pants. She wears no jewelry; she doesn't need it. Mama looks best in black, very fair and very striking. She knows this. Mr. Honeycutt seems mesmerized by the top three buttons on her blouse—they are open, and you can see the milkiness of her throat and neck.

Daddy's bustling around, pouring drinks for everybody. "Lana, what can I get you?"

"Oh, just seltzer water for me, Billy," Mrs. Honeycutt says, smiling slightly. Her teeth look like they've been dipped in tobacco juice. I bet she's a smoker. To Mama, she confides, "I'm watching my weight."

"Of course," Mama says, smiling back. Then she lifts up her wineglass and says, "Cheers to that, Lana."

Mrs. Honeycutt titters, and Daddy laughs, too loudly.

"That's a gorgeous bracelet, Lana," Mama says, leaning closer. "Wherever did you get it from?"

Beaming, Mrs. Honeycutt says, "I ordered it from the Avon catalogue last Christmas. Did you know they sell jewelry, too?"

"Well, no, I sure didn't," Mama says. She turns to us then. "Girls, did you know that?"

Celia and I murmur that no, we did not. We exchange uneasy glances across the room. Then Daddy starts on about some project at work, and Mama goes to the kitchen to check on the turkey. She is gone a long time. When she comes back, she says just a little longer.

We sit in the den for over an hour. I can hear Micah's stomach grumbling from across the room. Celia hears it too, and she presses her lips together tight to keep from smiling. I can't help it; I snicker out loud.

Daddy shoots me a warning look, but I can tell from the way his eyes are crinkling that he's trying not to snicker too.

By the time we get to the dining room table, we're all starved. Daddy says grace, and then everybody tucks into the food. The turkey's a little dry, but with gravy on top, who can really tell? Tastes fine to me. The potatoes are cold from sitting out so long, but you just pour on some of that hot steaming gravy and it heats them right up.

"Grace, everything is just wonderful," Mrs. Honeycutt gushes, dabbing a napkin to the corners of her mouth.

Mr. Honeycutt says, "Yeah, you are really somethin,' Grace. You have really outdone yourself. Everything's delicious. Right, son?"

Micah grunts and shovels a forkful of potatoes into his mouth.

"Micah, are you and my Celia in any of the same classes at school?" Daddy asks, gnawing on a turkey leg. He looks like he should be wearing a robe and a garland on his head like the Ghost of Christmas Present.

"Daddy, I'm a junior," Celia says, rolling her eyes. She looks at him like, *I can't believe you're my father.* Celia can say a lot with her eyes.

"Well, I know that, Celia," Daddy says, turkey leg midair. "Of course I know that."

Rolling her eyes again, she says, "So Micah's a freshman."

"Oh," Daddy says.

Mama snorts loudly. She's not eating much of anything. But she's drinking enough for everybody at the table. I think she's been drinking all day.

I say, "Well, Micah could be in accelerated classes, Celia. It's not impossible for the two of you to be in some of the same classes. Like, when I'm a freshman, I might be able to take—"

Celia kicks me under the table, hard. I stop talking and stuff some more turkey in my mouth.

To Micah, Daddy says, "Have some of that good dark meat, son. It's not as dry." He piles turkey on Micah's plate.

Mama says, "More wine anyone?"

"I'd love some, Grace," Mr. Honeycutt says, pulling at his shirt collar. He's sweating, and his face is getting redder by the minute.

Mama smiles at Mr. Honeycutt like he is the best-looking man in the room and not the color of a rotten tomato. She pours him a glass of wine, smiling all the while. Then she fills her own glass to the top, and drains half of it in one swallow.

"Hon, I think you may have had enough to drink tonight," Daddy says, forcing a jovial laugh. My stomach tightens, and suddenly my appetite is gone. I feel like I'm gonna throw up. It's one thing for Mama and Daddy to snipe at each other when it's just the four of us, but it's a whole other thing to have an audience. I wish the Honeycutts would disappear and take me with them.

The whole table has gone silent, waiting for Mama to answer. The Honeycutts are staring down at their plates, pushing food around. I guess they aren't used to a Wilcox kind of Thanksgiving. Celia and I are plenty used to it. We look at each other from across the table, and with her eyes, she says, *I hate them both.*

At this moment, I do too.

It feels like hours before Mama says, "Oh, I haven't had nearly enough, darlin'." She smiles and lifts her glass to Daddy. "Not nearly."

Just then, we all cringe. Even Micah.

I think I liked Thanksgiving dinner better when it was KFC.

After the Honeycutts leave, I sit at the top of the staircase with Meeks and listen to Mama tear into Daddy. Meeks rests his head in my lap, and I stroke his ears until he falls asleep.

"How dare you embarrass me like that! How dare you!" Mama's voice is uneven, shrill. I can hear that she's had at least two gin and tonics since supper. At least.

She rails on and on. "You humiliated me in front of our guests! The guests that you invited without even consulting me, the guests that I had to cook and clean for like a damn workhorse!"

"Grace, you were damn near drunk. What would you

have had me do? Carry you from the dining room table?" He sounds tired. He always sounds tired when they fight.

"Oh, shut up. You have no right to say a damn word to me. You hardly even live here, remember, Billy?" Mama's voice has taken on that screechy, desperate quality my father can't stand. I hate to hear her sound that way too. And it's always about the same thing: When are you coming home, Billy? Why aren't you here more often, Billy?

When Daddy's not around, she never sounds like that. Desperate, I mean. I know it's a terrible thing to say about your own father, but sometimes I wish Daddy wouldn't come home at all. Then Mama wouldn't always be waiting for him; she wouldn't be upset when he never came. She'd know not to wait. Then there might be some peace in our house.

I start to tiptoe back to my room, but the floorboard creaks, and Mama calls out, "Shug?"

I stand very still. Then she calls again. "Shug, is that you?"

"Yes, Mama."

"Come down here, baby." I hear Daddy mutter, "Let the girl sleep," but I come anyway. I have to.

Mama's on the couch, and Daddy's in his special

recliner chair. "Sit down a minute," Mama says, reaching out to me.

"Mama, I'm really tired. Can't I go back to bed?"

"Just sit down next to your mama a minute." She pats the cushion next to her, and I know there's no use fighting it.

I sit down, and Daddy shakes his head. "Don't bring her into this, Gracie."

She ignores him. "Shug, don't you think your daddy was way outta line tonight? Don't you think he just about ruined Thanksgiving dinner?" Her breath is hot, and I inch away from her.

"Mama, Thanksgiving dinner wasn't ruined. . . ."

"You can be honest, Shug. It's okay. We all worked real hard to make Thanksgiving dinner just right, and then your daddy went and ruined it." She glares at him, hard.

"Just stop it, Gracie. I mean it; I'm not in the mood for this." He takes a drink from his glass of watery bourbon.

"I'm havin' a conversation with my daughter. Feel free to leave. Feel free to go back to Atlanta for all we care, right, Shug?" Mama turns to me again, and tips my chin up. "We don't need him, do we, Shug?"

Daddy slams his glass on the coffee table so hard the

table shakes. "Enough!" I stay still, hardly breathing. "Annemarie, go back to bed."

I look at Mama, and she nods slightly. Hesitating, I stay put until Daddy barks, "Now, Annemarie!"

Running up the stairs, I can hear them going at it again. It looks like it'll be a headphones night.

chapter 24

I got my period in French class today. We were conjugating the verb to swim when I had to excuse myself and go to the girls' bathroom. For one horrifying moment, I thought I'd had an accident in my pants. When I realized what it really was, I wanted to cry. I think I did, a little. All I could think was, it's too soon. Everything has happened so fast. My whole life is changed, and I'm not even done being a kid.

Then I wadded up some toilet paper and stuck it in my underpants. In the hallway, I passed by Kyle Montgomery and Hugh Sasser and all I could do was nod stiffly. Could they tell? Did they know?

When I returned to French class, I asked Madame

Turner if I could talk to her in private. She said oui, and we went out to the hallway. I said, "Madame, I—"

"En français, mademoiselle."

"But, madame, I—"

"En français." She crossed her arms and waited.

"Madame, je . . . j'ai . . . I just got my period. Can I borrow a pad? S'il vous plaît?"

Madame Turner looked startled. "Er . . . Is this your first time, Annemarie?"

"Yeah. I mean, oui. C'est mon premier temps."

"Why don't you go to the nurse's office? I'm sure they can help you there."

The nurse's office? I mean, come on. I wasn't bleeding from anywhere I wasn't supposed to be bleeding from. It's a period, not a gash on the head.

So then I trudged over to the nurse's office, and Nurse Dewitt gave me a pad the size of a jumbo box of Kleenex. Wearing a diaper like that, how could a girl ever forget about her period? The rest of the day I walked around knowing it was there, knowing it would come again the next month, and the month after that.

I feel like my childhood has been ripped away from me, and now things will never be the same. *I'll* never be the same.

I've gone too far, seen too much; there can be no turning back now. I feel betrayed by my own body. I don't want this! I'm not ready for this! How come I don't get a say?

On the bus, I tell Elaine my news. Her face lights up, and she is so excited. It's like I've won the lottery or something. She clutches my arm. "Annemarie," she says, "You're *so* lucky!"

"Lucky? This isn't lucky. This is sucky."

"It's not like you didn't know it was coming. You should feel happy. You're an actual woman now. You're not a kid anymore."

"I'd rather be a kid any day."

"Don't be so ungrateful. It's a milestone, a mark of womanhood." For the first time ever, I see envy in Elaine's eyes, and that's when I realize that I have something she doesn't.

"Well, I don't want it. You take it. I'll be glad if it never comes back. I just want things to be like the way they were."

Impatiently she snaps, "Things can't stay the same forever, Annemarie. People change; they grow up. That's the way it's supposed to happen."

"I don't care. I don't want to change; I want to stay the same. Forever." And I mean it too.

Elaine makes a face. "Sometimes I don't get you at all."

Sometimes I don't get me either.

chapter 25

I think Elaine's breaking up with me.

After my last class I went to meet Elaine at her locker the way I usually do, but Hugh was already there. They were laughing and carrying on, but when they saw me, they hushed up like they were members of some secret club.

I said, "Hey, y'all." I stood there, shifting my book bag from one shoulder to the other.

Hugh nodded at me, and Elaine said, "Hey, Annemarie. I'm not riding the bus today. Hugh's going to walk me home."

"Oh. Okay, then. Call me later."

Elaine nodded and threw me a quick, excited smile.

Then they walked down the hallway together and I watched them go.

Sitting on the bus alone, I can't help but wonder if this is the beginning of the end for Elaine and me. It took me my whole life to find a best friend like Elaine. What would my life be like without her? She's already picking Hugh over me. If she doesn't call tonight, I'll know that we really are in trouble.

Instead of going straight home, I stop by Mark's house. For old times sake. He wasn't on the bus, and I know he didn't have to stay after school for practice, so I figure he must've left early. A dentist appointment, maybe.

For maybe the first time ever, I ring the doorbell. I'm not sure why. For some reason it doesn't feel right to just walk in anymore.

Mrs. Findley answers the door. She looks surprised to see me, but happy, too. Wiping her hands on a towel, she says, "Annemarie! Sweetheart, I've missed you. Mark's not home, but you come on in and chat with me."

My hand on the screen door, I falter. "Mark's not home?"

"No, dear, I dropped off him and some of his friends at the arcade after school."

"Oh," I say. I take a step back. "Who? Kyle and Jack?"

"Well, Kyle, but not Jack. Mairi and Hadley, too," she says. "I was wondering why you didn't go, Annemarie. We hardly ever see you anymore."

Mairi and Hadley? Since when do they go to the arcade with boys? They hate the arcade; they think it's boring. They don't even know how to play Skee-Ball. I know it couldn't have been a double date or anything. I bet they invited themselves along so they could drool over Kyle playing that free throw basketball game. What a couple of idiots.

Later that night Elaine calls me.

"I think Hugh's going to ask me out, Annemarie."

"Ask you out where?" I'm being obtuse on purpose. Obtuse means thick-headed or slow. It's one of Celia's SAT words.

"You know what I mean."

"Well, what are you going to say?"

"I'm going to say yes, duh!"

Picking my nails, I say, "I thought you weren't completely sure how you felt about him."

"When did I ever say that?"

"I don't know, but you did."

"Well, I'm sure now. I like him."
"All right, if you're sure."
"I'm sure."
Sure. Whatever.

chapter 26

I always wonder how people get together. How does it happen? Exactly what is said, or decided on? I wish I knew.

Mairi and Kyle are officially a couple now. I guess that afternoon at the arcade was their first step toward becoming boyfriend-girlfriend. They must have figured out that it was their destiny to be together, the prettiest girl and the prettiest guy. Everyone knows that that's what's supposed to happen. They owe it to the rest of us. Good-looking people are supposed to be together, like Barbie and Ken. It's, like, a law.

Mairi and Kyle aren't the only ones. Elaine and Hugh are a couple too. He walks her home from school, and I miss sitting with her on the bus. But the worst part is the way she thinks I don't understand her anymore. She'll get this faraway look in her eyes and say, "Sometimes I really miss Hugh." And I'll say, "But you just saw him at school." And then she'll say, "Oh, you couldn't understand, Annemarie." What is it I can't understand exactly?

And I haven't just lost her to Hugh. Now that Mairi and Kyle are a couple, the four of them probably do coupley things together. I bet they go to the movies on Saturday nights, and afterward they go to Mr. Boneci's diner. They probably share banana splits and feed them to each other like a bunch of monkeys. Elaine's not even allowed to date yet, so she tells her parents she's with me.

Celia has a boyfriend too. His name is Eli Parker, but everyone calls him Park. He's tall with shaggy brown hair, and his jeans are always dirty. I bet he never washes his jeans. He's the lead singer in a band called Rapid Dominance. Every day, it's Park this and Park that. "Park's got a gig at a bar in Patan County." "Park wrote me a song called 'Celia, How I'd Love to Feel Ya'." "Park wants me to go cross-country with the band this summer." Park makes me want to puke. He's always hanging around, like the weird smell in our basement. Where did it come from, and how can we get rid of it?

And it's not just Park or Eli or whatever his name is. *All* of this love crap makes me want to puke. Things were so much easier when it was just me and Celia and me and Elaine. Come to think of it, things were easier when it was just me and Mark, too. But the old me and Mark, without any of the love stuff. Life was simpler. Life was riding bikes and kickball and cherry Popsicles. There was none of this boyfriend-girlfriend business to mess everything up.

But then sometimes I can't help but wish I was a part of something too, a half of a whole. Elaine thinks I don't understand, but the truth is, a little part of me does. A little part of me does want someone to hold hands with and talk to on the phone late at night. But it's just a little part of me. The rest of me isn't ready. I don't know if I even want to be ready.

When I get home from school, Celia and Park are sitting at the kitchen table eating oranges. He's got his feet on the table, and he's throwing sections into her mouth.

Celia says, "Hey, Shug. Have an orange."

"Hey, kid," Park says. "Think fast." He throws a piece of orange my way, and it lands on my shoe.

"No thanks." Who does he think he is, offering me my own oranges in my own house?

Park shrugs, picks up the orange, and pops it into his mouth. "Waste not, want not."

"You're so gross," Celia says fondly. She scrunches her nose up at him, and he leans forward and kisses it. Then she giggles. I am so sick of hearing her giggle like that. I never knew my sister was one of Those Girls, those girls who giggle over every little thing.

"You're both gross," I say, taking an orange and walking up to my room.

After Park leaves, Celia comes up to my room and plops down on my bed. She flicks my wrist and says, "You wanna go to the movies tonight?"

I look up from my social studies book, surprised. This is awfully generous of her, seeing as how she's been spending every spare minute with Park. She never has time for me anymore, but I'll take what I can get. "I guess so," I say. We can share a box of Milk Duds and a large popcorn, extra butter, and we can throw it at people who talk during the movie, the way we always do.

"Good," she says, standing up. "I'll tell Park to pick us up at eight."

I deflate like an old birthday balloon. "Park's coming too?"

"Well, yeah." Celia looks mystified, like duh, of course he's coming too.

"Oh. Well, maybe you two should just go by yourselves then." I turn back to my social studies homework.

"What? Why? Don't you like him, Annemarie?" Celia sits back down again.

"He's all right."

"Park is more than all right, Shug. Oh, Annemarie, he's the best. He's wonderful. You've just got to give him a chance, and then you'll see." She falls back onto the bed, and her hair fans out on my pillow. "I really want you to like him. It was his idea that we all go out tonight, you know."

"It was?"

"Yeah. He wants to get to know you. I think I love him, Annemarie, I really do. I think this is real."

I stare at her. This was the first she'd talked of love. "How do you know?"

"You just do." She props her head up on one elbow, and says, "I love him so much it hurts sometimes."

"It hurts?"

"Mmm-hmm." Her face is soft and dreamy and full of secrets, and I know why Eli Parker loves my sister.

"Well, how do you know it's not just puppy love?" I say meanly. Something in me wants to squash those stars in her eyes.

"It's not." She looks dreamier than ever.

"Do you think he loves you, too?" I already know the answer. Of course he loves her. I'd seen the way he looked at her, the same way every boy looked at her, including my boy. My Mark.

She thinks this over. And slowly Celia nods. "Yeah, I think he does. And I don't know if it'd really matter if he didn't."

"Are you crazy? Of course it matters! I couldn't love somebody who didn't love me back a trillion times more." A lie. Hadn't I been loving Mark all this time and hadn't he been not loving me back?

"You'll understand one day, loving somebody so much you just want to be near them 'cause they make you feel so good." Celia sits up and hugs her knees to her chest. She looks about six years old. "He makes me feel like I'm the only person in the room."

"He loves you, Celia."

She looks so pleased, I feel like Cruella DeVille for trying to steal that look in her eyes. "You really think so?"

"Yeah." Of this, I am certain. Who could know my sister and not love her?

chapter 27

In the middle of the night I wake up to hear Mama and Daddy fighting. I try to fall back to sleep, but it's useless. I get up instead. I make my way through the darkness, and it's Mama's voice that guides me. When I get to the stairs, I stop and rest my head against the wall. It sounds like the same old fight.

"I work, Gracie, that's what I do."

"Work, work, work. That's all you ever do, right, Billy?"

"Darlin', one of us has to."

"And just what do you think I do?"

"You turn the TV off and on at a nursing home."

"Damn you! Who do you think keeps this family together while you're gone *workin'*?"

"To be honest, I don't really see you overtaxin' yourself. You let both of those girls run wild while you lay around like the Queen of friggin' Sheba. Lord only knows where Celia spends her nights, and Annemarie never even leaves the house."

This stings. I didn't think anyone had noticed the way I was always at home. I can't help it if everyone I know has taken up arms in the sexual revolution. You'd think he'd be relieved, grateful even.

Mama laughs bitterly. "Oh, please. It's a little late for you to be taking an interest in the girls. Pardon me, Billy, it's a little late for you to be taking an interest in *our* girls. Other girls, you've got interest aplenty. Why, you've got interest just shootin' right out of you—"

"I'm not having this conversation with you, Gracie."

"Oh yes, you are," Mama hisses. Her voice drops low, and I can't hear what she says next.

Then he says, "Frankly, I'm surprised you even noticed." His voice is so cold I don't recognize it as my daddy's. "I'm surprised you were sober enough to notice anything at all."

The sound of Mama's hand across Daddy's cheek slices through the air. It's loud enough to make me jump.

"Don't do that again, Gracie." The quiet warning in his voice silences the whole house. So does the door he slams.

I hear the car start, drive away. And then all I hear is Mama crying. My shoulders feel tight, and I just want to go back to sleep.

It wasn't fair of Daddy to say that about Mama never being sober. Plenty of people drink. That doesn't make them alcoholics. If that were true, Clementon would just be one big AA meeting. And it's not like she drinks all the time. There'll be times when she won't drink anything for days. Mama will go to work and then she'll come home, and sometimes she'll even make supper. Or she'll go out with Gail, or help me with my homework. I don't really need her help anymore, but it's nice to work together on something. It's nice to have her help me. To sit with her in the dining room and have her hair fall across my cheek and breathe in her perfume. It's like she's a real mom.

And then Daddy will call and ruin everything. He'll say he's not coming home that weekend, or he *will* come home and they'll fight the way they always do. Then she'll drink. Sometimes it's like there's this well of sadness inside her, and she has to drink to fill it up. And then sometimes it's like there's a monster inside of her, and drinking's the only thing that will calm it down. And sometimes she drinks just because.

When I was little, it wasn't so bad. Or maybe it was and

I just didn't notice. It didn't occur to me to wonder why she woke Celia and me up in the middle of the night to make strawberry sundaes. Or why we were the only kids I knew who didn't have a bedtime. Or why we were allowed to eat whatever we wanted whenever we wanted. I could have sour cream and onion chips for dinner and Mama wouldn't bat an eyelash.

That's probably why I like vegetables so much. The other kids used to be so jealous when I'd pull a bag of chips and a box of cookies out of my lunchbox, but what I wouldn't do for a Ziploc bag of cut celery or baby carrots. I used to trade Mark my chips for his fruit. Most times it was sliced apples or a banana, but on lucky days there was a kiwi or a tangerine.

When you're little, lots of things slip past you. Not anymore. I'm old enough to know that not everybody's mama drinks and not everybody's daddy is never home. Some daddys are home for dinner every night, like Mr. Findley. Not my daddy, though.

They haven't had a fight this bad in a while. I wonder if I should go down and comfort her. The thing is, I'm sick of it. I'm sick of the fighting and the crying and the drinking, and I wish I didn't have to be a part of any of it. But I am.

When I walk into the kitchen, Mama's standing by the sink wiping her eyes with a paper towel.

I say, "Is everything okay?"

She looks plenty sober now. Her eyeliner is smudged, and her face is red, but she's still the most beautiful woman I know. Painting a bright smile on her face, she says, "'Course, Shug. Daddy and I just had a little fight. Go on to bed; everything's fine now."

"You sure?" Pretending to believe her is easier than not.

"'Course I'm sure. Git on now; scoot."

I walk back up the stairs, but instead of returning to my room, I go to Celia's instead. She's asleep in her bed, and I push her over and crawl in.

My feet are cold, so I warm them up on the backs of her legs. "Annemarie," she growls.

"Hmm?"

"Get your feet off of me before I cut them off."

"Sheesh. Sor-ee." She's falling back to sleep again, and I whisper, "Celia . . ."

Silence. "Celia . . ."

"*What?*"

"Do you think Mama and Daddy are gonna get divorced?"

"No."

"Do you think they should?"

"Go to sleep, Shug."

"I'm not sleepy."

"Well, I am. So shut up or get out."

I shut up.

chapter 28

Daddy called this morning. I picked up the phone as usual. He told me he wasn't coming home today the way he was supposed to. Something came up at work, something real important. With Daddy, it's always something "real important." I asked him if he wanted to talk to Mama; he said no, he'd call back later. I used to be disappointed when he didn't come home. Now I'm not even surprised. I'm even a little relieved. But what does surprise me is the way Mama still gets upset. You'd think she'd be used to it. But every time he does it, her face crumples for a second, like she's breaking into little pieces. Pretty soon there'll be nothing left of her.

This afternoon Jack left a note in my locker. It said, "Can't tutor at my house today, I'll be at your house at

7:30." It's just like him to change things up on me like that with no notice. Luckily Mama's working tonight, and Celia's hardly ever around anyway, so we'll have the house to ourselves.

As soon as I get home from school, I start cleaning up the house like a madwoman. I wash the dishes that have piled up, I put away coats in the closet, I wipe down the counter, I even dust the TV. I don't know that the TV has ever been dusted.

For dinner I fix myself two boiled hot dogs and cold baked beans. With ketchup. Plus root beer. It's a feast fit for a king.

After I eat, I set up a workstation in the dining room. I lay out paper and mechanical pencils, and at 7:30 on the dot, the doorbell rings.

I run over to the front door, and it's Jack. On time. I can tell that he's just had a shower because his hair's still wet. His hair looks so dark it's almost black. He just stands there, shifting his weight from foot to foot. "Hey."

"Uh, hey, come on in."

Leading him through the kitchen, it hits me how weird it is to have a boy that's not Mark in my house. It's like on those standardized tests you take at school—which of these things does not belong? Jack Connelly, that's what.

"You want somethin' to drink?"

"Nah."

"Well, let's get to work then."

Jack grins and salutes me. "Sir, yes sir."

I make a face, but I'm not really mad. We sit down at the dining room table, and the two of us get straight to work.

I'm explaining what a split infinitive is when Mama waltzes into the room. She's wearing her silky emerald green nightgown, and I already know something's wrong. Her eyes look glassy and unfocused, and my heart almost stops when I realize she's been drinking. Not a little, but a lot. "Mama, I thought you were at work." My voice comes out sounding highpitched and worried.

"I wasn't feelin' so hot this mornin'. Can't a girl take a sick day?" When she's been drinking a lot, she talks extra slow. That's how you know she's in a bad way: She sounds like the South.

Mama zeroes in on Jack. "Hi, there. Who's your little friend, Shug?"

"Mama, this is Jack Connelly. You've met him before. We go to school together."

"Hello, Mrs. Wilcox."

"Jack Connelly . . . Hi, darlin'. Your mama works at that

steak restaurant over on Clinton Boulevard, right?" She beams at him.

"Yes, ma'am." I've never seen Jack so polite. He's acting as if everything is normal. He's acting like he's come to pick me up for the prom and he's tryin' to make a good impression on my folks.

"Your mama and I go wayyy back. She had her eye on my Billy, you know. So did just about every girl at Clementon High School." Mama giggles. "But I got him, yes siree. And your mama, well, she was just fit to be tied . . . Trish, whatever happened to her? She took up with that no-account fool Glen after graduation. And then he up and left her, didn't he?"

"Yes, ma'am, he did."

"I tell you, Jack, Trish is better off without a man. Men'll just break your heart. Don't you grow up and be a man, y'hear?"

"No, ma'am."

In a low voice I say, "Mama, we're trying to get some work done. Will you please just go back upstairs and leave us alone?"

"Now, Shug, don't you go gettin' uppity with me." She smiles winningly at Jack. "This one over here thinks she's the Queen of Sheba. . . . Are you two hungry?"

"We're fine," I say through clenched teeth.

"Now don't be rude to your little friend. Jack, are you hungry, darlin'? Wouldn't you like a 'lil snack?"

"No, thank you. I already had dinner."

"All right then." Her gaze wanders around the room, then refocuses on the two of us. "Are you two gonna be all right alone in here?"

Oh God, no. This is every nightmare I've ever had, times a million. "*Yes*, Mama." With my eyes I beg her to leave, but she doesn't seem to see me.

She winks at Jack. "Can I trust you alone with my Shug? I know how boys your age think."

"We're just friends, Mama," I hiss. I glare at her so hard it seems to wake her up a bit.

She nods. "All right, all right. Nice to see you, Jack. Say hello to your mama for me." She goes back upstairs without another drunken word.

For a long time neither of us say anything. Tears are pricking the backs of my eyelids, and I'm afraid to speak. I'm afraid that if I open my mouth, I'll start bawling and everything inside of me will come out.

Finally I manage to croak, "Sorry about my mother. She didn't mean any of it. She just gets like that when she drinks." I've never been able to say those words to anybody, not even Elaine. Especially Elaine. But somehow, I knew I could say them to Jack. I sort of needed to.

Jack shrugs and grins at me. "Aw, that was nothin'. My dad could be a real asshole when he drank."

"Yeah?"

"Oh, yeah. He'd get in these tempers, throw stuff around. Once, he threw me down the stairs. That's how come I had a cast on my leg back in fourth grade."

"I thought you said it was 'cause you were poppin' a wheelie on your bike."

"Nah. I just told everybody that 'cause it sounds better than gettin' thrown down the stairs by your drunk dad." Jack grins again, but it's not his usual grin, cocky and sure of himself. This grin is empty and sad. "But everybody knew anyway, right?"

I don't say anything. All of the neighborhood kids knew that Jack's dad knocked him around sometimes. There was getting in trouble once in a while, and then there was getting beat up, and Jack got beat up.

"Who cares. It was a long time ago. He doesn't even live with us anymore, and he stopped drinking anyway. Well, he says he has. He says he's changed. He goes to AA and stuff. My mom and Clarice go visit him sometimes."

"What about you?"

"I say, once a deadbeat, always a deadbeat." He looks away. "But maybe one day, you know? He's been helping my mom out with bills and stuff for a while now, so maybe he really has changed. Anyway, your mom's not so bad, Annemarie. I remember that time she was one of the chaperones for the circus field trip back in third grade. She wasn't supposed to buy us any popcorn or cotton candy, but she did anyway."

"Yeah, I remember." I'd been proud of her that day. She'd worn a blue-and-white-striped sweater and blue slacks, and she'd been prettier than every other mother there.

"And she used to come to those pickup softball games in the park. She'd bring Styrofoam cups and a big jug of Kool-Aid, and she'd cheer you on."

"I remember."

"She's a pretty cool lady."

"When she isn't drinking."

"Yeah, well, that's more than some people." For someone who's not so good with words, he knows exactly how to say the right thing. Which is a whole lot more than some people.

When I see Jack at school the next day, I'm only a little bit embarrassed. It's like we share a secret. I know he won't tell anyone about Mama, and he knows I won't say anything about his dad. When he sees me in the hallway, he says, "Hey, Einstein" and that's it. It's like nothing happened.

But something did happen, and part of me is glad. Part of me is relieved. Somehow, saying it out loud makes it all feel a little less terrible. I know Celia'd probably be mad at me for telling, but it's not like I had a choice. He saw it all with his own two eyes. He was a witness, and I'm not even ashamed.

At dinner that night I don't even look at Mama. But I do eat her chicken à la king. There's corn pudding, too, and ice cream for dessert. Rocky road.

chapter 29

Elaine and I are sitting in science class when we hear the announcement. It's the end of the day, and whoever's on the PA system is going on and on about school spirit and picking up trash. No one pays attention until we hear the words "seventh-grade dance." "Clementon Junior High will be having its annual seventh-grade dance this month. It will be held on the second Friday of the month. You'll get more information in your gym class, where you will have a lovely dance unit. And girls and boys, please note that this is not a formal dance. Churchgoing attire will be just fine, and formal wear would be incredibly inappropriate. On that happy note, have a nice afternoon!" The bell rings and everyone makes a rush for the door.

A dance.

Mama tried to teach me how to dance when I was seven. Celia was eleven, and of course she already knew how. She was born dancing. It was after supper, and I was trying to watch cartoons. Mama suddenly got it into her head that I *simply had to learn how to dance*. It was all very life and death, and if I didn't learn right that very minute, well, it would just be tragic for all concerned. She said that all Cavane women could dance. I said I'm not a Cavane, I'm a Wilcox, so it doesn't matter.

She cranked the stereo up high, and Nina Simone's growly voice filled the whole house. Mama dragged me off my feet and said we'll fox-trot first. She danced me around the living room, and I just couldn't get the hang of it. I couldn't find my rhythm; I couldn't hear the beat. I was just trying to keep up, and I couldn't. Next we tried the waltz, and I couldn't get that, either. It was the going backward part that messed me up the most. But Mama just kept whirling me around like she couldn't hear me.

She had been drinking that night; of course she'd been drinking. Her breath was hot on my cheek when she said, "Two left feet, just like your daddy. You really are a Wilcox, Shug." My eyes burned, and I snatched my hands away. I said, "I don't want to dance with you anyway."

Celia had been reading a book in the tatty old armchair, and when Mama said, "Celie baby, come dance with your mama!" she leaped up and danced like the Cavane she was. They did the Lindy Hop, and both of their feet moved just the way they were supposed to.

My feet don't move the way they're supposed to. How in sam hill am I supposed to go to a dance?

As Elaine and I walk to the bus loop, I say, "A dance sounds dumb."

"Are you kidding me? A dance will be the funnest thing that's ever happened in this town!"

Geez. I thought we'd had some pretty fun times too. "I don't know. It'll probably be lame. I doubt I'll even go."

"Don't be crazy. Of course you're going. You could ask Mark. It'll be fantastic," she says. Her eyes are glazed over, and I know she's picturing herself in some strapless dress with a corsage on her wrist. "Your big chance for him to finally notice you."

"Uh . . . I don't know." I don't know if having Mark notice me is worth having to go to a dance. "Might not work."

"Oh, it'll work all right." She puts her arm around me. "We're gonna make you hot. He'll fall all over himself when he sees you."

Well, that doesn't sound so bad. Sounds pretty good, actually.

Elaine volunteers to chair the decorations committee, and like a shot, Hugh says he'll cochair it with her. Hadley's in charge of refreshments with Mark, and Mairi's heading up music with Kyle Montgomery. The dance committees read like a who's who of Clementon Junior High. Guess who I am. Nobody. I'm not on any of the committees.

When I can't fall asleep at night, I close my eyes and picture how I want the dance to go. We're in the gym, and a slow song comes on. Maybe "Crazy Love" or "Unchained Melody" or "I Only Have Eyes for You." Yeah, definitely "I Only Have Eyes for You." He pushes his way through the crowd, and there I am, swaying to the music by myself. He says, "Annemarie, will you dance with me?" I say okay, and he takes my hand and leads me to the dance floor. And I put my arms around his neck, and then we're swaying together. He's holding me tight, and he keeps looking at me like he can't believe what he's seeing, what's been right in front of him all along. Me, Annemarie Wilcox.

chapter 30

Mama's missing.

Before I left the house this morning, I told Mama that I needed a ride home from school today because of French club elections. Normally I'd ask Celia to swing by and get me in Margaret's car, but Celia'd gone away on a camping trip for the weekend. Anyway, Mama said no problem, she'd be there. She wasn't there. Everyone else's parents came to pick them up at 4:00. I stood at the bus circle, waiting for her, knowing she wasn't coming, but waiting all the same.

When it started to get dark, I gave up and walked home. It's a long walk when it's just you and your thoughts. I was really steaming by the time I finally got home, planning out how I was gonna yell at her, how I was gonna make her sorry. But then I saw that Mama's car wasn't in the driveway.

For two hours I paced the living room floor, watching the clock. Ever since I was little, I had a fear that Mama might get into a car accident and never come back home. An irrational fear, Mama calls it. Doesn't seem so irrational to me. There've been times when she had a little too much to drink and she still drove anyway. Nothing stops her when she gets it in her mind to do something.

It's late now, and I'm not mad anymore. I'm just scared.

With Celia on a camping trip, the only person I can call is Mrs. Findley. She'd help me. She'd know exactly what to do. But Mama would hate her knowing our business, and to be honest, I'm not too keen on the idea either. Maybe before, it would've been okay, but not anymore. It's not that I don't trust Mrs. Findley, because I do, maybe more than any other adult I know, but I don't want her thinking badly of Mama. Or of me.

There's only one thing I can do. I've gotta call Daddy. Mama could be hurt somewhere. And if she's not hurt, if she's off having fun, then maybe she deserves to get in trouble. I could've been kidnapped or run over or worse. It would've been all Mama's fault. I almost wish I was kidnapped or run over or worse; that way she'd feel awful. Like the worst mother in the world.

I dial the numbers slowly, giving myself one last chance to back out. I tell myself maybe she's called him already, and everything's fine.

He picks up on the third ring. "Bill Wilcox," he says.

"Hi, Daddy. It's me, Annemarie." Your daughter.

"What's going on, Shug?" He sounds busy, distracted.

So Mama hasn't called him. This could be good or it could be really, really bad.

"Nothing . . ."

"Good, good. Listen, I'm on another call, so I can't talk just now. We'll talk when I come home next week, okay?"

"You were supposed to come home today."

"Change of plans. There was a meeting I couldn't get out of. Didn't your mother tell you?"

"She must have forgotten."

"Ah, well. We'll have us a good visit when I come home next week. I'll bring you something extra special. Listen, I've really got to get back to work, Shug. Give Celia and your mama kisses for me. And one for you, too."

"Okay . . . Daddy?"

"Yeah?"

"Daddy, Mama hasn't come home yet."

Silence. "What do you mean, she hasn't come home yet? Is she still at work?"

"No . . . She was supposed to pick me up after school, but she never came. I'm worried, Daddy."

He sighs and says, "Annemarie, I'm sure she's fine. She probably just got caught up somewhere. You know how your mother is."

"Daddy, she could be hurt. She was supposed to pick me up hours ago." I am waiting, waiting for him to say sit tight, I'm on my way.

He doesn't say it. He says, "Where's your sister?"

"On a camping trip. Daddy, maybe you should come home. Something could be really wrong." I pause carefully. "She could've had an accident or something. A car accident."

Daddy curses under his breath. "That woman . . ."

I wait. I've planted the seed; he's worried now. Even though he's mad, he's worried, too.

"Sit tight, Annemarie," he says at last. "I'll be there as fast as I can."

It takes about three hours to get from Atlanta to Clementon. Daddy makes it home in just over two. Mama still hasn't come back. We sit on the couch and wait.

"It's just like your mama to pull something like this," Daddy says, twisting his tie loose.

I'm starting to regret this already. "She might be hurt somewhere, Daddy."

He just shakes his head.

Mama comes home around 2:30 a.m. She is drunk. When she sees Daddy sitting on the couch, her happy smile fades. She looks confused. "What in the world are you doin' home, Billy?"

"I'm home because our daughter called me," Daddy says. He's so angry, his voice shakes. "Annemarie was worried sick."

"Gail and I had a drink after work," Mama says, her hand fluttering to her forehead. The confusion is gone, and defensiveness is starting to creep into her voice. "I'm sorry you came all this way for nothing. Annemarie, I told you I'd be home late tonight. Why did you go calling your daddy?" She looks at me like I've betrayed her, like I'm not her daughter anymore.

My mouth is dry. Licking my lips, I say, "I-I guess I forgot."

Daddy stands up and strides over to Mama in two big steps. He looks like he wants to shake her, like he's *going* to shake her. "She walked home from school in the dark!

You were supposed to pick her up from school! Do you know what can happen to a child in the dark, Grace? *Do you? Do you even care?*"

Mama looks at Daddy like he's slapped her. "Of course I care!" She looks at me then, eyes pleading. "Shug, baby-doll, I'm sorry. I just forgot."

Before I can speak, Daddy says harshly, "You're pathetic."

Jumping up from the couch, I shout, "Don't say that to her! Don't you say that to her!"

"Annemarie, go to your room," Daddy says, in a low voice. It is an order.

"No," I say. My fists are clenched at my sides. "You don't get to tell me what to do."

"I told you to go to your room," he says. Every word is clipped, precise. "I'm not going to tell you again."

He's so angry, I'm scared. Scared of my own daddy. But I don't move. "Why should I? I can hear you two up there, too, you know."

"Annemarie," he warns. The muscle in his jaw is twitching.

"Go on, Shug," Mama says. "I mean it; go upstairs. This is between me and your daddy."

I look at her then, really look at her. To her I say, "You know what? You're both pathetic."

Then I run upstairs and slam my door. As soon as the door closes, I start to cry. I went and told on Mama. Now everything's wrong.

They fight for a long time. I lay there in the dark, listening for as long as I can. I hear Mama say, "If you hate your life here so much, you should just stay gone."

I don't move. I wait to hear what he'll say next.

(Don't go, don't go.)

Daddy says, "Darlin', I'm not the one who hates her life. That's you. You're the one who can't stand to be here."

That's about all I can take. I reach for the headphones on my nightstand and turn my music up loud. I fall asleep and dream and dream.

Daddy's gone when I wake up. It's like he was never here at all.

chapter 31

After school Elaine and I are in my bedroom doing homework, and she says, "So Mairi invited us to sleep over on Friday. Do you want to go?" She fingers the lace edge on the quilt Grandma Shirley made me when I was born.

I look up from my math worksheet. "She invited us or you?"

"She invited both of us."

"Who else did she invite?"

Elaine ticks the names off her fingers. "It's gonna be me, you, Jo Jo Washington, and Hadley." Jo Jo Washington was the queen bee at Lincoln Elementary, and Mairi has deemed her cool enough to hang with us. I think Jo Jo is a dumb name, almost as dumb as Jo Jo herself.

"Have fun," I say.

"Come on, Annemarie. Do you want to go or not?"

"Not."

Elaine sighs. "Mairi's really not so bad when you get to know her."

"How would you know? You're the one who doesn't know her. I've known her my whole life, Elaine. Don't tell me I don't know Mairi Stevenson."

"Fine. Forget it."

"You go. I'll be busy anyway."

"Busy doing what?"

Busy picking hair up off the carpet. Busy de-ticking Meeks. Busy counting my freckles. Busy feeling sorry for myself.

"Celia and me are doing something."

"Annemarie, you're a lousy liar. Come on. Let's just go. Please? I don't want to go without you."

I don't want her to go without me either. But.

Being the girl at the slumber party no one wants around is a terrible thing. She's the one the mom has to befriend. She's the one no one wants to sit with at dinner, or split the last piece of pizza with. She's the one the other girls whisper about when she goes to brush her teeth. ("She's so annoying . . . No offense, Annemarie.") She used to be Sherilyn, and I can't let her be me.

If I go to Mairi's sleepover, I know that I'll be the one shunted off to Siberia, sleeping on the cot while everyone else doubles up on Mairi's twin beds. I know because once upon a time, Sherilyn slept on the cot while I got to sleep under Mairi's patchwork quilt. And the worst part is that I didn't even care that Sherilyn was all alone. You can't afford to care; you've just got to enjoy your time at the fair and be glad. I was glad I wasn't the one on the cot; I was glad I wasn't the one who didn't have someone to whisper with as we fell asleep.

But what will happen if Elaine goes to the sleepover without me? What if they seduce her with their sparkly nail polish and their Truth or Dare? Then I'll be the one left behind. I'll be Sherilyn.

"Fine. I'll go. But I'm telling you, it won't be fun."

chapter 32

Mairi Stevenson is adopted. Not a lot of people know this. I only know because Mama told me. Mairi sure lucked out when she got Cal and Lindy Stevenson for parents—the Stevensons are rich folk. They're richer than anybody I know. Ever since we were little, Mairi talked about her debutante party, and how she was going to have her gown flown in from Paris. How there would be a band, how she would wear silk stockings, how everyone would be jealous because her debutante party would be the grandest party Clementon ever saw. How only the prettiest and most popular girls would be invited. She said that if I promised to buy a nice dress and curl my hair, I could come too. I promised. We were seven then.

The Stevensons live in the nice part of our neighborhood, just the three of them in a five-bedroom house. Their brick house is on a hill, and their paved driveway looks about a mile long. They have an outdoor hot tub and a workout room for Mrs. Stevenson.

Mairi has two rooms: one bedroom and one "office" for her books and her computer. It used to be her playroom. That's where she kept her dollhouse. She had a gigantic dollhouse that used to be her grandmother's. It had real wallpaper and fancy brocade furniture and even miniature Monet paintings on the walls. I used to love to play with that dollhouse. I'd pretend that I lived in the house with my pretend family. My mother, Beth, my father, John, and my brother, John Junior. It just about broke my heart when Mairi decided she was too old for a dollhouse and Mr. Stevenson had to put it away in the attic. I wanted to ask her if I could have it. I'd have traded Meeks for that dollhouse. But Mrs. Stevenson's allergic to dogs. And anyway, you don't go around asking people for a family heirloom, no matter how badly you want it.

chapter 33

Mrs. Stevenson is a good cook. She makes special sleep-over food for Mairi's parties—caramel popcorn, mini gourmet pizzas, macadamia double-fudge brownies. Even though I didn't want to go to Mairi's sleepover, I was still looking forward to the snacks. I should have known Mairi is now too grown up for junk food. On the marble-topped kitchen counter, Mrs. Stevenson has set out a platter of raw vegetables, bags of rice cakes, and fancy bottled water.

There's a great big Christmas tree in the living room. It's so tall it touches the ceiling, and the ornaments are navy and silver. No homemade Popsicle-stick ornaments for this tree. Not like the Findleys, with their cinnamon and apple-sauce cookie-cutter ornaments and their popcorn on a string, and their rag-doll angel that sits on top. But at least the Stevensons have a tree. We don't. Mama thinks it's silly, commercial.

Mrs. Stevenson's on the phone when I get to Mairi's house, and she's all dressed up. Her hair is curled in an updo, and she's wearing a silky black tank top and white pants. She waves at me to sit down as she makes a face into the phone. "Suzy sweetie, I've got to run. There's a thing at the club tonight, and of course Cal and I have to make a little appearance. . . . I'll call you later, hon."

Hanging up, she says to me, "Miss Annemarie, it has been far too long, darlin'. How have you been? How's your mama? Is she doin' all right?"

Mrs. Stevenson makes me nervous, always has. My palms are sweating as I say, "I'm fine, Mrs. Stevenson, just fine. Mama's fine too."

"And that handsome daddy of yours?" She winks, resting her elbows on the kitchen counter.

"He's good too."

"Well, you tell them both that Lindy and Cal say hello."

The doorbell rings then, and Mrs. Stevenson rushes off to get the door. She returns with Elaine, who sits in the chair next to me. Elaine and I sit at the kitchen table like two inmates waiting to be released for good behavior. My hands are in my lap, and I'm sitting straight as an arrow.

Mrs. Stevenson says, "The other girls have gone with Mr. Stevenson to rent some movies. They'll be back any minute now." She beams at Elaine. "Elaine, I'm so thrilled you and Mairi have gotten to be friends. She's told me all about you. It was so sweet of you to have her over for dinner at your house."

I look at Elaine in surprise. When had Mairi gone to Elaine's house for dinner? And why hadn't she invited me?

"I told Mairi that she's so lucky to have a friend from a different culture," Mrs. Stevenson continues. "I want you to teach her all about where you come from. Maybe she could even learn some Chinese! Imagine that, my baby girl speakin' Chinese."

"Oh, I'm not Chinese, Mrs. Stevenson. I'm Korean, Korean American," Elaine says. "And I'm actually from New York."

Mrs. Stevenson's smile doesn't waver. "Well, *Korean*, then. You could teach her Korean."

Elaine smiles back. "Well, I'm not that great myself, but I could try."

Mairi and everyone come home then, and we all go upstairs. After we drop off our overnight bags in Mairi's room, she tells us that her mom and dad are going to a country club party and won't be back till late. She and Hadley exchange grins. Suddenly the air feels charged, and I have no idea what's coming.

We change into our pajamas—Mairi in a hot pink camisole set, Hadley in a crop top and boxer shorts, Jo Jo in a striped tank top with matching shorts, and Elaine in an oversized T-shirt with a ripped shoulder. Me, I'm wearing a white tank top I borrowed from Elaine and a pair of Celia's terry cloth shorts.

I haven't been in Mairi's bedroom in a long time, and there are little differences now. Your feet still sink into the marshmallowy pink carpet, she still has twin beds, but she has new sheets. There's a framed Degas print where her Beauty and the Beast poster used to be, and her collection of glass ballerina figurines is gone. Whenever I came to her house, I would count the ballerinas and name them— Suzette, Violetta, Antoinette, Bridgette, all fancy double-*t* names. I wonder where they went, if they're with that doll-house in the attic.

We're sprawled out on Mairi's twin beds doing our nails when Mairi jumps up suddenly. "Be right back, girls." She disappears.

"What do you think?" I ask, holding out my hands for

Elaine's inspection. The color is called Arabian Nights, and my nails sparkle like rubies. I hardly ever wear nail polish, and I can't stop looking at my nails.

"Hot," she says. Then she lifts up her hand—her nails are glittery pink.

"White hot," I say. "What's it called?" I like to know the names of things.

Elaine inspects the bottom of the nail polish bottle. "Disco Bubblegum."

"So, Annemarie, who do you like?" Hadley says suddenly. She and Jo Jo are sitting in the bed across from Elaine and me.

I swallow. "No one."

"That's not what I heard," she says, blowing on her nails.

I look at Elaine, who shrugs helplessly. "What did you hear?" I say. My heart is thudding loud as can be, and all I can think is, don't say Mark. Don't say Mark.

Hadley smiles. She is enjoying this moment, wielding this power over me. "I heard you like Jack Connelly. Is it true?"

Relief washes over me like a warm wave. "Ew. No way. I just tutor him in English."

"I think he's kind of cute," Jo Jo says. Then she sees

the look on Hadley's face. "What? What's wrong with him?"

"Are you kidding me?" Hadley shrieks. "He's *so* immature. He's like, total redneck trash. His dad's a drunk, you know. And his mother works at a *diner*. . . . No offense, Annemarie."

More than anything, I would like to throttle Hadley Smith. I would kick her butt clear across Clementon. I hate that girl something fierce.

The room has gone quiet, and everyone's waiting for me to say something. I say, "I already told you I don't like him."

Hadley squints her eyes at me. "Well then, who *do* you like?"

Then the door flings open, and it's Mairi with five cans of Budweiser. She sashays around the room, grinning widely and clutching the cans to her chest. Hadley squeals and claps her hands. "You're so bad, Mair!"

Mairi does a little dance and puts the beers on the floor. She pops off the tab and says, "Cheers, y'all."

I look at Elaine, but she just shrugs and smiles. She reaches for a can, opens it, and takes a swig. Elaine grimaces, but then she drinks more.

"All right!" Mairi cheers. They high-five, and Hadley

frowns. She grabs a can and takes a long drink, throwing her head back. Coughing, she throws a can to Jo Jo. Jo Jo looks uncertain for a moment, then follows suit. Everyone's laughing and drinking, and I just sit on Mairi's bed, arms wrapped around my knees, trying to make myself invisible.

Then Mairi looks at me, her glossy lips curved in a smile. "Your turn, Annemarie." It's a direct challenge, and every one of us knows it.

The last thing I want to do is drink. I've tasted beer before. It was late at night. I was thirsty, and I thought it was flat ginger ale. It tasted like bad medicine. No way do I want to drink that stuff again. No way do I want to be like Mama.

Every other girl in the room is staring at me, including Elaine. "What's the matter, sugar?" Mairi taunts. "Too chicken?"

Swallowing, I say, "No . . . I just don't feel well today. It'd probably be better if I laid off alcohol."

"Like you ever drink," Hadley scoffs, waving her Pretty in Pink nails in the air.

"I do so drink. I just don't feel like it tonight."

Rolling her eyes, she says, "Sure." She runs her hand through her streaky brown curls, searching for split ends.

She won't find any. Girls like Hadley don't get split ends.

"Annemarie, you don't have to drink if you don't feel like it," Elaine says. But her eyes are saying something else, and I can tell she wants me to. She wants me to be a part of the group almost as much as I want to be a part of it, and for some reason, this makes me mad. Why does she need this so bad? Why wasn't it enough when it was just me and her?

Mairi puts her arm around me. Her buttery blond hair smells like apples and Dove soap. "Hadley, it's okay if Annemarie doesn't want to drink. She's still too young." She releases me and smiles knowingly at the other girls.

"It's not that," I protest.

"Then?" She holds the beer in front of me, arm outstretched. "Come on."

Slowly I take the can from her. It is cold and sweaty. "Just a little sip then . . . Seriously guys, I don't feel good." Now I really do feel sick. The smell of the beer and the nail polish remover makes my stomach turn.

I put the top of the can to my lips and drink. It tastes bitter, and I feel hollow, like someone's spooned my insides out like a gourd. I wish I could spit it back out, take that moment back, do it over.

Everyone claps, and Mairi turns her stereo on loud. It's already forgotten. It never mattered in the first place. The girls start dancing around, and I sit on Mairi's bed watching them. Not one of them understands. They have no idea.

That night Hadley and Mairi sleep in one of the twin beds, and Elaine and I sleep in the other. Jo Jo sleeps on the cot.

It takes me a long time to fall asleep, but I do.

I wake up the next morning to the smell of frying bacon and the sound of Mrs. Stevenson shrieking. She's brought us a pitcher of orange juice, and she's found the empty cans of Budweiser. We forgot to throw them away; they're just lying there on the floor for all the world to see.

Everyone scrambles out of bed. "Mama, we were just playing around, we didn't really drink any," Mairi says.

"Don't you lie to me, Mairi Leigh. And to think your father and I trusted you. We trusted you girls to conduct yourselves as ladies, even with us gone." She shakes her head at us, and then her eyes land on me. Her thin lips tighten. "Girls, get dressed. I won't be telling your parents about this. We'll keep it our little secret, but this can never happen again, do you understand?"

Eyes lowered, we all murmur yes ma'am, we understand. Except for Elaine, who's from the North and never says sir or ma'am to anybody. "You, miss, are coming with me." She grabs Mairi's arm and marches her out of the room.

The rest of us stare at one another helplessly. "You think she'll tell our parents?" Jo Jo says, biting her lip. We sink back down onto the beds. Without Mairi, we don't know what to do.

Hadley's the first to recover. "No way. She cares too much about what the other country clubbers will think. She'd die if they found out."

"Are you sure?" Jo Jo asks.

"Yes, I'm sure," she snaps. "Now let's just get dressed and get out of here."

My mind is on that bacon. Mrs. Stevenson makes an incredible sleepover breakfast—bacon, sausage, eggs, pecan waffles. Restaurant-quality food. If I can smell bacon, she must have made all the other stuff too, Mairi's diet be damned. My mouth waters and I say, "But what about breakfast?"

Hadley looks at me like I'm the village idiot. "We're not staying for breakfast."

chapter 34

During lunch Jack got into a fight with an eighth grader. There was chocolate pudding everywhere. He got out-of-school suspension, and his mother had to come pick him up from school. I watched from the window in science class. I saw them walking to their car. Mrs. Connelly was wiping tears from her eyes, and Jack looked miserable. I felt sorry for him.

It's Jack's third fight this school year, and we're barely even halfway through. I really don't understand him. If he'd quit getting into fights and talking back to teachers, maybe he'd actually learn something.

After school I ride my bike over to Jack's with his assignments for the week. I only volunteered to do it because no one else came forward. And also, I feel sort of guilty for not sticking up for him at Mairi's sleepover. Not that he would ever find out about it, and not that I have any reason to stick up for him, but it was wrong of me not to say *something*. On behalf of his mama, at least. I could've told them that she doesn't work at a diner; she works at a *steakhouse*. And his daddy's in AA, which means he's not even a drunk anymore. I could've and should've said both those things, but instead I kept my mouth shut like a yellow-bellied coward.

When I pass Mark's house, he's shooting hoops in the driveway. I wave. It's the first time I've seen him at home in a long while. I'm really not planning on stopping, but *he* comes over to *me*. He's wearing a black T-shirt with the sleeves cut off even though it's pretty cold out. "What are you up to?" Mark asks, dribbling the ball with his left hand.

"Going over to Jack's house."

He pushes his hair out of his eyes and squints at me. "Oh yeah? You guys have tutoring today?"

"No, I'm just bringing his homework to him."

"I can't believe he was stupid enough to get into another fight. Sometimes he's a real idiot." He dribbles the basketball between his legs. "You wanna play Horse?"

"Nah, I gotta drop this off at Jack's."

"Aw, come on, just one game."

We end up playing four games, and by the time we're done, it's getting dark. I'm regretting volunteering to bring Jack his work for the week. Things feel so normal between Mark and me, and the last thing I feel like doing is trekking all the way over to Jack's house. Still, I gave my word.

Then I think of that sad look on Trish's face, and I pedal extra hard.

Jack answers the door. When I see his black eye, I don't even feel sorry for him. I just feel mad. I'd like to blacken his other eye.

"Here." I shove the stack of papers at him, hard.

"Thanks." He looks at me, and with his eyes he says it again, thanks.

Shaking my head, I say, "You know, you can't keep getting into fights over stupid stuff."

"Are you here to give me my homework or to nag me?"

"I'm just trying to help. You're gonna get really behind if you keep this up, Jack."

"That's my problem."

"It's my problem too, when I'm the one tutoring you! Sometimes you act like an idiot!"

Redness is creeping up his neck, and he says, "I'm really not in the mood for this today, okay? I feel bad enough already, I don't need you reminding me of what an idiot I am." His voice breaks.

I look away. I wish I was still playing Horse in Mark's driveway. "I said you act like an idiot, I didn't say you *were* one."

"My mom says that if I get into another fight, I'm gonna have to go and live with my dad." Baby tears are forming in the corners of his eyes, and he scratches at them like they itch. I look away again. Never thought I'd see Jack Connelly cry. I want to say the right thing, but what is the right thing?

I say, "Shoulda thought of that before you went and got into another fight."

Jack doesn't say anything, and it's so unlike him that I feel sorry, really sorry. I say, "Hey, let's study for that quiz, okay?"

"I don't really feel like it today," he says, his hand on the door. "But thanks for bringing my work."

"Aw, come on, Jack."

He shakes his head and shuts the door. And I'm left standing there, feeling like a real crumb.

chapter 35

The call comes that night, and as usual, I'm the one to pick up the phone. I swear, you'd think I was the only one in the family with hands.

"Hello?"

"Is that you, Annemarie honey?"

"Uh, yeah."

"It's Mrs. Findley, sweetheart. Is your mother home?"

"My mother?"

"Yes, dear. Is she at home?"

"Uh." What in the world could Mrs. Findley have to say to my mother? And furthermore, what would Mama say to Mrs. Findley? I am tempted to say no, Mrs. Findley,

Mama's left the state and has no plans of returning. Ever. "Yes, ma'am, just a moment."

Phone in hand, I sprint to the living room where Mama's lying down. "Phone for you, Mama." Her eyes remain closed.

"It's *Mrs. Findley*," I hiss.

Mama holds her hand out for the phone, and she doesn't open her eyes. "Hi, Helen," she says. "What can I do for you? I'm fine, thank you. Mmmhmm. Oh, I see. Well, yes, Billy probably will be away on business. But I'm sure I can make it. I'm always happy to help. . . . Yes, you too, Helen." Mama clicks the phone off.

"What's going on?" I demand. "What did Mrs. Findley want?"

Mama opens her eyes and says, "I'm going to help chaperone your dance."

WHAT? This time my heart really does stop beating.

She smiles tiredly. "There, aren't you pleased? Your mama's joinin' in and doin' mamalike things. Next thing you know, I'll be headin' up the PTA."

"I'm not even going to that dance," I say. "So thanks but no thanks."

Her smile fades. "What are you talking about? Of course you're going to the dance."

"No, I'm not. Dances are stupid. I'm not going."

Flatly she says, "You're going, Annemarie."

In my head I think, *Not if I can help it.* But I'm smart enough not to say it out loud.

chapter 36

At the lunch table Mairi asks me if my parents are getting divorced. She says her mother told her that my daddy was looking to get his own apartment in Atlanta.

I pretend not to hear her. I concentrate on eating my tuna fish sandwich, like it's the most important thing in the world, but inside it feels like something in me is breaking. Then she says, louder, "Annemarie, is it true your parents are getting divorced?"

It's like the cafeteria has gone silent, and all I hear is buzzing in my ears. In that moment, it's just Mairi and me. There's no one else at that table, just me and her. I feel like a skinny brown rabbit under Mairi's paw, and there's no way out.

Everyone stares at me. Even Elaine.

At times like these, you realize just how alone you are in this world.

I chew slowly, then finally say, "No. No, that's not true." My voice sounds quivery and weak, and I hate it. I hate everyone at this table. "They're crazy about each other. They're completely in love. Tell your mother to mind her own damn business."

Mairi's mouth falls open. "My mother says that your mother's a drunk, and that's why your father's leaving," she blurts out.

"Shut up. Shut your fat mouth. She's not your real mother anyway; your real mother didn't even want you."

Hadley gasps, and I almost gasp too. I can't believe those words just came out of my mouth. Mairi's gaping like a dying fish; her mouth opens and closes but nothing comes out. Her blue eyes look shiny, like she might actually cry. There, I've done it now. I've committed social suicide. I'm done for.

Shaking, I stand up and crumble my lunch bag into a tight ball. And then I walk away. I think I may have given up my seat at the lunch table for good.

Later that night, Elaine calls me.

"Mairi was way out of line," she says.

I don't say a word.

"We all thought so. After you left I told her she shouldn't have said it."

Silence from my end.

"I'm sorry, Annemarie. I should've said something right away; I was just so surprised. I mean, you never mentioned anything. . . ." Her voice trails off.

"That's because it's not true. Mairi Stevenson is a damn liar, and so is her mother." My voice breaks. "Everybody knows that Mrs. Stevenson's a liar."

"Okay, I'm sorry. I really am. Please don't be upset."

"I'm not upset."

"Okay."

"Okay."

"But . . . Annemarie, it was kind of harsh to bring up Mairi being adopted. You know she's sensitive about that."

"You knew too?"

"Yeah, she told me a few months ago."

I swallow. "Well, if everybody already knew, I don't see what the big deal was."

"Everybody didn't already know." She pauses. "Annemarie, she cried in the bathroom the whole lunch period."

I didn't know that. How could I have known that? The only time I ever saw Mairi cry was when Sherilyn accidentally broke one of her porcelain dolls.

"You sure she was really crying? She's a good actress, you know."

"Annemarie!"

"What? I'm just sayin'."

"She was really upset. Maybe you should talk to her."

"Got nothing to say."

At lunch the next day part of me wants to walk right on by their table, like I don't even see them. But I don't; the thought of sitting alone at lunch is more than I can bear. I wish I could be that brave. Instead, I sit down at the table and take every item out of my brown paper bag. Tuna fish sandwich again, bag of pretzels, two chocolate chip cookies, and a juice box. I stare down at my lunch, saying nothing.

Elaine says, "How was the math quiz, Annemarie?"

"Pretty hard." I look around the table, and everyone is silent. Mairi won't even look at me, and Hadley's glaring in my general direction.

The rest of the lunch period, the only person who talks to me is Elaine. Two tables over, Sherilyn sits with Carol

Motts and Dana Toto. Their heads are bent close together, and they're giggling. Carol and Dana aren't cool. Carol's strict Southern Baptist, and she isn't allowed to wear pants, so she wears culottes instead. Culottes aren't cool. The boys call Dana "Toto," and they bark at her when she walks down the hallway. Not cool either. But at this moment I'd give anything to be sitting over there with them, giggling with our heads touching.

Sherilyn looks up and sees me watching her. I smile. She gives me a half smile and then returns to their conversation. I wish she'd have gestured for me to come over, and I wish that I'd have been able to do it. But I wouldn't have, and I guess she knows it.

As we're leaving the cafeteria, Hadley grabs my arm. "We haven't forgotten about what you did yesterday, Annemarie," she hisses.

I say nothing.

"You owe Mairi a huge apology." Her brown eyes narrow. "Are you even sorry?"

"Yes." Not that it's any of your business.

"Then tell her."

"Well, is she sorry for what she said to me?"

"What she said to you wasn't nearly as mean as what you said to her. Anyway, she was just asking you a question. You didn't have to bite her freakin' head off." She rolls her eyes. "Look, if you want to keep hanging out with us, you better apologize to Mairi."

Satisfied, she releases my arm and walks away.

After school I ride my bike over to Mairi's house. As I walk up her paved driveway, my heart hammers in my chest like a little brass drum. What if she slams the door in my face? What if Hadley's with her? I can't face the both of them.

I ring the ivory doorbell, and a minute later she opens the door. Just Mairi, holding a piece of peanut butter toast in one hand. I thought she'd stopped eating carbs.

"What do you want?"

She's not going to make this easy. "I came over here to say I'm sorry."

Her lips are clamped shut. I go on, "I shouldn't have said what I said. It was none of my business."

She nods, and quickly I add, "But you shouldn't have said what you did about my parents."

Mairi shoves the rest of the peanut butter toast into her mouth. She takes her time swallowing. She doesn't look at me when she says, "I know."

chapter 37

The dance is all anyone can talk about. At the lunch table Mairi announces that her dad offered to rent them a stretch limo, but she declined of course, because "limos are so tacky."

After school at Jack's house, we're working on vocabulary lists when he bursts out, "What's the big deal about this stupid dance? I mean, who cares? People act like it's the prom or something. Not that prom's such a big deal either."

I am amazed, because for once, Jack Connelly and I are in complete agreement. "I know. It's because they have nothing better to get all worked up about. At lunch today, Mairi was talking about *limos*."

Jack snorts. "Mairi Stevenson is braindead. I don't know why Kyle likes her."

"Duh. 'Cause she's pretty."

He shrugs dismissively. "Yeah, she's all right."

"Oh, come on. Every guy at school wants to be with Mairi."

He shrugs again. "Not every guy. Mairi's good-looking, but her personality's kinda foul. She's overrated." I try to hide my smile. "Hadley, too. I mean, her body's all right, but she has a horsey face. I don't know why Mark asked her to the dance."

My smile disappears. I feel like he just socked me in the stomach, hard. "Mark asked Hadley? Hadley Smith?"

"How many Hadleys do you know?"

"Why would he do that?" I can hear a loud buzzing in my ears, and my chest feels so tight. How could this have happened? I knew they'd been hanging out, but this . . . this was more than I could take. Mark Findley has been mine my whole life, and all of a sudden Hadley decides she wants him? How can that be right?

"That's what I'm sayin'. . . ." Jack peers at me. "What, do you like Mark?"

"No . . . I was just wondering. . . ."

He's grinning slowly. "Because if you do, I'd be happy to set you two up—"

"Are you deaf? I said I don't like him!" I snap, flipping through my language arts textbook. My face feels hot. I know that I have to get out of this room fast. "Look, are we done here?"

"I guess so," he says. "So are you gonna go to the dance?"

"No. Are you?"

"No way."

As I bicycle home, it starts to rain, cold, almost-snow kind of rain, and I'm glad. I can blame my wet cheeks on the rain.

Every morning, I dread going to school, because it's just another day of not being asked. Every morning, someone new has a date. "Have you heard? Junie just asked Pete, and he said yes." "Colbert's taking Regina." I paste a knowing look on my face and pretend I already know all about it. And then, "Who're you going with, Annemarie?" Airily I say, "Oh, I doubt I'm even going. Dances are so lame. I probably won't even be in town."

There's only one person I'd want to go to this dance with, and it looks like it's too late. He's asked Hadley Smith of all people. And if I even go to the dance, which I'm not, I'll be stuck with Mama.

chapter 38

Mama insists on taking me shopping for my dress. I kept telling her I wasn't going, but she wouldn't listen. I finally caved in, and I was hoping she'd slip me a fifty and let me go with Celia, but something's come over her, and she wants to be a part of my big night. I'd planned on buying a dress from the sales rack and spending the rest on books. Not that I'm even going.

Saturday morning she drives me over to Bodewell's Department Store. I begged Celia to come with us, but as usual, she's too busy for her only sister. She and Park went to see some garage band in Patan County.

Mama strolls around Bodewell's like she's Mrs.

George T. Bodewell herself, and I trail after her. For someone who's usually so thrifty, she seems to care an awful lot about this dress. Money is no object, she declares.

She picks up a red dress with a heart-shaped neckline and black velvet polka dots. No way do I have what it takes to fill out that dress. "Forget it, Mama," I say. "You can just put that back, because there's no way I'm even trying it on."

"It's cute, Shug. We'll set it aside as a maybe." She throws the dress over her arm.

"Mama, I said no. . . . What about this one?" I point to a navy tank dress made of rayon. It's on sale. . . . Maybe she'll buy me some books with the leftover money.

"That looks cheap. It's too plain."

"I like it."

She ignores me and continues wandering around the store. I go to the dressing rooms, sit down cross-legged on the floor, and open up my bruised copy of *Tuck Everlasting*. I'm on the third chapter when Mama reappears with an armload of dresses. On top is a pale pink dress with spaghetti straps and bows. It looks like a frilly cupcake. It's the kind of dress Celia would have worn to her seventh-grade dance.

"Go try these on." She thrusts the pile of dresses at me, and I can already feel my skin getting itchy.

"Those don't look right."

Mama exhales loudly. "If you don't like what I picked out, why aren't you helping me?"

"I already told you I don't want to go."

"Do you know how much I would've loved it if my mama took me shopping for a new dress? Do you?"

"That's you," I say. I'm gripping my book so hard my hand is sweating.

She clenches her teeth. "There's just no pleasing you these days. You never used to give me any trouble. You left that to your sister. *Now* look at you, Miss Mary Mary Quite Contrary."

"I'm not being contrary! I told you I didn't want to go! You're the one who won't listen! You never listen!" This comes out louder than I intended.

Mama stares at me like she's never seen me before. "Fine," she says tightly. "We're going home."

I sigh. "Just forget it. I'll try them on."

"No, give them to me." She takes the dresses and throws them on top of the clothing rack in a big heap. "We're leaving."

She doesn't say a word to me the whole way home.

shug

After dinner that night, Mama calls Mrs. Findley and tells her something's come up at work, that she won't be able to chaperone the dance. I feel guilty, but I'd be lying if I said I wasn't relieved, too.

chapter 39

Mama doesn't speak to me all weekend. Oh, she speaks to me, but not really. She says turn the TV down and have you done your homework yet and pass the pepper. But that's it. She doesn't bring up the dance once. I know she's waiting for me to apologize, to tell her I want her to buy me a dress and that I really do want to go to the dance.

The worst part is, I do sort of want to go to the dance. A little. The more people talk about it, the more I want to go. I don't want to be left out. I don't want to be the only seventh-grade girl who doesn't go to the dance, well, the only one other than Carol Motts, whose parents are super-strict and won't let her go to any kind of dance. I want to wear a pretty dress and I don't want to be "just Annemarie." I want to be special.

But now it's too late. Some mean, sharp little part of me can't let Mama have this. It means too much to her, and I don't want her to take any bit of pleasure in it. I want this to be all mine, and if it can't be, well, then I guess I won't be going. Not that anyone would care. Elaine's going with Hugh; Mark's going with Hadley. Who will notice if I'm not there?

On Sunday night, the three of us—Celia, Mama, and me—are sitting in the living room. This is a miracle in and of itself, because Celia's nights are reserved for Park. But tonight she is home, painting her nails candy apple red and watching TV. Mama's sitting in an armchair reading the newspaper, and I'm sprawled out on the couch feeling as low as I've ever felt.

At the commercial break, Celia says, "Sit up, Annemarie, and I'll do your nails for the dance tomorrow night."

Hope surges through me. Right now, if Mama were to say, "Oh, Annemarie, just do us all a favor and go," I could sigh and say, "Fine, I'll go already." I peek at Mama, who doesn't look up from her paper. She turns the page, and it feels like an eternity before she speaks. "Annemarie's not going to the dance," Mama says. "She thinks dances are stupid."

"Oh, of course you're going, Shug. Don't be such a baby." Celia grabs my left hand and I snatch it away.

"I'm not going," I mumble. Just this once, can't Mama be the grown-up? Can't she be the one to give in?

"See?" Mama says. "She's not going."

I should've known. I've never been able to beat my mama at anything. She always wins. If I go to the dance, she wins, and if I don't, she wins.

chapter 40

The dance is tonight. Kids at school were yakking it up about the dance all day. I couldn't wait to get home. The only thing that kept me going was the thought of crawling under my covers with some hot chocolate and a good book.

Elaine kept saying that I should just come alone, that tons of girls were going stag, that it wasn't a big deal. Not a big deal—ha! Last I heard, even Sherilyn had a date. Martin Lum asked her. Martin with his thick glasses and his greasy nose. Heck, I'd have gone with Martin Lum if he'd asked me.

I'm lying in bed reading when Celia struts in. I snarl, "Ever heard of knocking?" but I stop short when I see what's in her arms.

It's a dress. It's black with tiny ribbons for straps, and a full skirt with crinoline underneath. You couldn't buy this kind of dress at the mall. It's old, and it's sassy and it's sophisticated. It's like nothing I've ever seen, not up close, anyway.

"Where'd you get it from?" I breathe.

"It was Mama's," Celia says. "I found it in one of her old trunks."

"Where are you gonna wear it?"

"I'm not wearing it, dummy. You are." She holds the dress out to me. "You're going to that dance, Shug."

I can't stop staring at the dress. It is perfect, just right. "I told you I wasn't going."

"Shut up and try it on."

"It'll never fit me." I reach out to touch it, and I listen to the way the fabric whispers.

Celia says, "We'll make it fit."

"Does Mama know you have it?"

"No. Who cares? She's not gonna need it tonight. What, does she need a party dress to drink? I don't think so." We giggle, and she hands me the dress. "Try it on, Shug."

"But I don't have a date."

"So?"

"So I'm not like you." I stare at the carpet, then look up at her. "Celie, nobody asked me."

She shrugs. "So what? You should be grateful you don't have a date. This way, you can work the whole room and you won't have some little dweeb hanging on to you. Now try it on, for God's sake."

I try it on. It hits just below the knee. It fits.

Celia decides that my hair should be down. She curls it and brushes it till it shines. She puts mascara on my lashes and peachy pink blush on my cheeks. She dabs lip gloss on my lips and shimmery powder all over my face and collarbone. Last of all, she sprays me with her perfume. She never lets me use her perfume. It smells like ripe pears and vanilla.

Celia's all smiles, and she keeps saying see? See? I do see. Celia can make anything come true. When I see myself in the mirror, I can't believe it. I don't look like me at all. I look pretty. I look like the kind of girl who deserves to go to a dance. Celia's lent me her red wool dress coat with the Peter Pan collar, and I'm even wearing heels! Celia borrowed a pair from Margaret for me—they are black with high, high heels and a dainty toe. She tells me to be careful with them, because they are Margaret's lucky shoes. They'll bring me luck too, she says.

When I am finally ready, Celia calls Park to come pick us up. We wait for him in the kitchen. Then Mama walks in, and Celia and I both stiffen. I feel like I've been caught going through her purse.

She stares at me. At the dress, and then back at me. "Nice dress," she says.

"Thanks. It's yours."

"I know." We look at each other some more. Then Park's car honks, and Celia says it's time to go.

Mama hesitates, and then she says, "Shug."

"Yeah, Mama?" I hold my breath.

Please don't let her try and come too. Please don't let her ruin this for me.

"I'll pick you up after the dance."

"Okay," I say.

I hope that she can see the thankfulness I feel in the way I smile at her, but I don't know.

Celia and I run out the front door, and as I'm climbing into the backseat of Park's car, I look back. Mama is standing on the front porch watching us. Beautiful, she mouths. I feel like I could cry. For the first time ever, I feel it. Beautiful, I mean.

chapter 41

The gym looks like a Christmas tree. Elaine's done a really good job. Twinkle lights are strung all around the room, and sparkly streamers and glittery confetti too. There's a shimmer in the air, and I know that this is my night.

Elaine rushes over to me as soon as she sees me come in. "Annemarie! You're here! I love your dress!" she shrieks. She is wearing a strapless yellow dress and a flower in her hair. It is a white calla lily.

We hug. "I'm so glad you came," she whispers.

"Me too," I say. She takes me by the hand, and we walk over to Mairi and Hadley. They are standing by the punch bowl. Mairi is wearing that black and red polka dot dress Mama wanted me to wear, and Hadley is in a hot pink halter dress. It's tight, and it shows off every curve she's got. They both look suspiciously tan.

Mairi looks me over and says, "I like your dress. Where'd you get it?"

Hadley says nothing, just watches me with narrowed eyes. Her silence is proof positive that Celia did somethin' right.

"Thanks," I say. "It's vintage." I don't know if it's vintage or not, but it sounds good and Mairi looks impressed.

"So where are the guys?" I ask, supercasually.

Mairi rolls her eyes and flicks her hair in the direction of the basketball court. I look over. Mark, Jack, Hugh, and Kyle are trying to slam-dunk balloons into the hoop. I laugh, and Mairi frowns.

"I want to dance," Mairi says, her lower lip sticking out. "Come on, girls. Let's go make them dance with us."

She marches over to the boys, and Hadley and Elaine follow her. Elaine gestures for me to come too, but I shake my head no. They pull their dates by the arm and onto the dance floor, and soon they're all dancing in a circle.

Pouring some punch into a paper cup, I remind myself that I wanted to come, that being alone isn't really that bad.

Then Jack walks over to the punch bowl. "Hey," he says.

He is wearing a white button-down shirt, black pants, and sneakers. And a tie that says, "Eat my shorts."

"Hey," I say.

"I thought you said you weren't coming."

"I thought you said *you* weren't coming."

He shrugs and tosses a cookie into his mouth. "My mom made me," he mumbles, his mouth full.

"You're gross," I say, curling my lip at him. "Learn some manners."

"You're gross," he mimics.

And then we stand there and eat cookies. Occasionally we laugh at people dancing, and Jack imitates their moves with a deadly serious expression on his face. He moves back and forth, shuffling his feet and waving one arm in the air. "I'm Kyle, and I'm cool," he says. I can't stop laughing.

I also can't stop watching Mark. He and Hadley seem so comfortable with each other. She keeps giggling and messing with his hair, and he lets her. He actually lets her. I know for a fact that he doesn't like anyone touching his hair.

Every so often Elaine raises her eyebrows at me, and motions that I come over and dance too, but I shake my head. I'm fine where I am.

Then Ms. Bickey gets on the microphone and

announces that it's the last dance. I haven't danced with Mark once, or anybody for that matter. This is my last chance. He's standing across the room with Kyle and Hugh. I think all the girls made a group trip to the bathroom, and I figure I have a few minutes at least.

To Jack I say, "I'll be right back."

He just shrugs, and I make my way over to the boys. Kyle looks at me with wide eyes. His eyes flick up and down like he doesn't recognize me. I almost say it's me, Annemarie, you big dummy. But the fact that he notices, that feels really good.

Kyle clears his throat. "Wow, you look nice," he finally says. He is wearing a pink tie with light blue stripes. Only Kyle Montgomery could wear a pink tie.

"Thanks," I mutter.

I look only at Mark when I say, "You wanna dance?"

Mark looks surprised, but he nods. I take his hand, and we walk out to the dance floor, and it's just like I imagined. I'm careful not to look in Jack's direction; I don't want to see him making fun of any of *my* moves. My arms are around Mark's neck, and I'm careful not to let any part of me get too close to any part of him, but it's nice. He's wearing his father's cologne, and his shirt feels crisp against my fingers. We're swaying more than we are dancing, but it's still nice. I'm also taller than Mark, taller than I'd realized. But like I said, it's still nice.

It's nice until I feel the tap on my shoulder. It's Hadley. "Excuse me, but I'm going to have to cut in, seeing as how Mark's my date and all," she says. She smiles without opening her lips.

Mark doesn't say anything; he just shrugs. I don't know what to do, so I back away.

As I lean against the bleachers, I watch them dance. Hadley's a good head shorter than Mark. Her arms are wrapped around his neck, like she's hanging on for dear life. She looks up at him, and then he kisses her. Just like that, they're kissing.

I feel dizzy and sick to my stomach. We were supposed to be each other's first kiss, and now everything's ruined. And the way they're kissing, it doesn't look like it's the first time. Ms. Bickey goes over and says something to them, and they stop. For the second time that night, I feel like I might cry. When did Mark stop being mine?

I just want to go home. My feet hurt. So much for Margaret's lucky shoes.

chapter 42

After the last dance everyone's scrambling to get their coats from the bleachers. I'm in the very back, sorting through a pile of coats when I hear his voice, the voice I'd know anywhere.

"Annemarie? Come on, she's barely even a girl."

"She looked like a girl when you were dancing with her a minute ago." It's Hugh. He's making kissing noises. "Oh, Annemarie, I love you, baby."

"Shut up. I only danced with her because I felt sorry for her. She doesn't even know how to *dance* like a girl."

Laughter.

It's Mark, my Mark. He's standing with Kyle, Hugh, and Jack.

My insides freeze up, and I can hardly breathe. I can hardly see. I hate him, hate him, hate him. I hate them all. I want to curl up and hide so no one ever sees me again. I want to make him hurt the way I hurt. I want to die.

I must have made some sound, because he looks up and sees me standing there. His mouth hangs open, but no words come out. We stare at each other, and it's like the whole gym has gone silent and there's nobody there but us. Just me and Mark. Except, there isn't a me and Mark anymore.

I open my mouth to speak, but somehow, I can't think of a single thing to say.

He says pleadingly, "Annemarie." That's all, just my name.

I shake my head. Then tears blur my vision, and I walk away before he can see me cry. Slowly, until I am out of the gym and out of sight, and then I pick up speed. I run like Satan is hot on my heels.

I run all the way to the parking lot, where Mama is waiting. The car is parked in the front row, and I climb into the passenger side without a word.

I forgot my coat, too.

Mama doesn't seem to notice my hunched shoulders,

how small I am. How small I feel. Shivering, I keep turned away from her and cry the whole way home. I pray please don't see me, please just don't. Please oh please. I concentrate on those words and will myself to forget everything else. This is the worst night of my life.

He doesn't like me. He never liked me. He never will.

Worst of all, he is ashamed of me.

As soon as our car pulls into the driveway, I run out and into the house. I run all the way to my room and, kicking my shoes off, I fall onto my bed. Under my quilt I curl up like a sick kitten, and I cry. I cry and cry and cry. It's the kind of crying where you can't breathe it hurts so bad— your chest heaves and your eyes swell, and you can't stop for all the trying in the world.

It hurts bad. I keep hearing the words—"barely even a girl," "felt sorry for her," "barely even a girl." Over and over they dance around my head like a merry-go-round. I keep seeing them on the dance floor, kissing like they really know each other. And Jack standing there, not sayin' a word, and here I was thinking we were almost friends. He's not my friend, not even a little bit. He's not my friend, and Mark's not my friend, and Elaine's barely my friend. I've never felt so alone in my whole life.

Later I hear my bedroom door open, and Mama comes

in. She sits on the edge of my bed. "Annemarie, what's the matter?"

Right now I don't trust my voice to speak. I just shake my head. She doesn't move, so finally I say, "Nothing. It's nothing. Just leave me alone." Tears drip down my cheeks, and I wipe them away with the back of my hand.

Mama smoothes the hair away from my forehead. "Shug, tell me what's wrong." Her breath is warm and sweet, and I start to relax against her fingertips.

She keeps smoothing my hair, and finally I feel brave enough to whisper, "Mama, he doesn't want me. Mark doesn't want me."

Her hand stops moving. "Then he's a fool. You are really somethin', Annemarie. You are extraordinary, and if Mark Findley can't see that, well, then he's a young fool."

I roll away from her and stare at the crack in my wall. "I hate it when you say that."

"When I say what?"

"When you say that I'm extraordinary."

"Why? It's God's honest truth."

For a moment I don't say anything. Then I finally say, "You just think I'm special because I'm *your* daughter. It's because you think *you're* special. You don't see me. You just see yourself."

She says nothing for a moment, and then, sharply, "Look at me."

I don't move.

"Annemarie, I said look at me." Her tone doesn't leave room for argument.

Heaving a great sigh, I turn and look at her. My mother's face is grave, and I see that I've hurt her. For once I'm the one doing the hurting, and I'd thought that was Daddy's job.

"Is that what you think?"

I shrug.

"You have been special your entire life. You were born that way. They put you in my arms, and you were already your own person, and I knew it. I knew you were somethin' special." Her gaze is soft on me for a moment, then it turns back to hard emerald, and I wonder if I imagined it. "Shug, if you can't see your own worth, you sure as hell can't expect someone else to."

"I know what I'm worth."

"No, I'm not sure you do." She pauses. "People are gonna disappoint you sometimes. We're flawed creatures. Not one of us is perfect, not even you, and you've gotta let people mess up and then you've gotta forgive them. That's just life."

"I know all about people disappointing me. You do it all the time."

Mama flinches, and part of me is sorry, but the other part is glad. Glad that I've hurt her. "How do I disappoint you?" she asks. Mama looks so small, and for the first time, I feel powerful. I feel like I could hurt her some more.

"You disappoint me when you drink. You disappoint me when you drink so much you forget about Celia and me. You disappoint me when you drink so much you embarrass me in front of my friends or when you forget to pick me up places because you're too drunk or too hungover." Every word feels like a dart in my hand, and I hit the bull's-eye each time.

She closes her eyes briefly, and I know her pain is real. It's one of the realest things about her. "I'm the only mother you've got, so I guess we're just gonna have to make the best of it."

I know that this is the closest she will ever come to saying sorry, and I know that things aren't going to change. That's just life. My life, anyway.

"I'm sorry." And I am. Not sorry for what I said, but sorry for why. Having my feelings hurt by Mark Findley isn't a good enough reason for being mean on purpose.

"Hush." Mama leans close and kisses my wet cheeks.

"You were lovely tonight. There just aren't enough words, Shug."

Then she says what she's said to me ever since I was a baby. "You're my sweet Shug, my little bowl of sugar."

Tears spring to my eyes again. I haven't heard Mama say that in a very long time. Maybe because I haven't been her little bowl of sugar lately. I haven't been very sweet at all. I'd forgotten how special it made me feel whenever she said it.

Then Mama leaves and closes the door, and I can still smell her perfume.

chapter 43

When something that terrible, that horrible happens to you, you don't want to talk about it with anyone. You want to bury it deep inside you and let it rest in peace. You want to forget it ever happened. You want to stay home from school.

Come Monday morning I tell Mama that I have a stomachache, and she says people who don't face their problems head-on are the worst kind of cowards. I say that I really do feel sick, and I even manage a tear or two. She sighs and says oh, go back to bed. I practically sprint up the stairs.

I spend the morning watching trashy TV, and then I fall back to sleep.

When I wake up later that afternoon, my eyes are

swollen and Elaine is sitting on the edge of my bed shaking my shoulders. "Wake up, Annemarie!"

"Elaine, what are you doing here?" I sit up and she releases me.

"Are you okay?" She peers at me closely, like she's looking for bruises, for any sign of permanent damage. I'm afraid I'm already damaged for life.

"I'm fine, why wouldn't I be?" I pull the covers up to my chin.

"Everybody's talking about it."

Everybody knows? Dread seeps into my bones. "Talking about what?"

"How Jack pushed Mark into the bleachers over something he said about you."

WHAT? "WHAT? Jack did what?"

"He shoved Mark, and then Mark shoved him, and then Mark was lying flat on his back." A giggle escapes from her pink lips. "It was kind of funny."

I lean back against my pillows, and a smile sneaks across my lips. Mama and I were watching an old movie once, and the two guys fought over the girl. They threw punches and everything, and Mama said there's nothing quite like having two boys fight over silly little you, is there? At the time, I agreed, but I didn't really understand what she meant. Now I know, a little. The warm feeling spreads across my chest like a sunburn: two boys fought over silly little me. Well, maybe not *over* me, but *because* of me, and that's better than nothing.

"He got out-of-school suspension."

"WHAT?"

"Yeah, for starting the fight. God, he's so immature. Even the other guys say so. He likes you, you know."

"Who?"

"'Who?'" she mimics, grinning. "You know who. Jack."

"You're crazy. We're barely even friends. Why do you always have to turn everything into a teen drama? It's not always about that."

Elaine looks taken aback. "But he does like you, Annemarie. It's not just me. Hugh thinks so too—"

"Oh, and if Hugh says so, then I guess it must be true, right?"

"Well, yeah, in this case." She stares at me. "What's your problem?"

"This isn't an after-school special, Elaine. I'm not gonna pair off with that idiot Jack Connelly just because everyone in Clementon has to be boyfriend-girlfriend all of a sudden."

She narrows her eyes. "Everyone, or me?"

"Just forget it."

"No, I don't want to forget it. I want to know what you meant by that."

"Fine!" I burst out. The words erupt out of me like hot fizzy soda spilling all over the place. "Hugh's all you ever talk about! You used to be interesting! Now you're so wrapped up in your little 'relationship' you can't even think about anyone else."

Elaine stands up jerkily. "I came over here because I was worried about you."

"Yeah, right. You just wanted to have something to report back to your queen, Mairi. All you think about is yourself."

"You're the one who can't think about anyone else! You're the one who's selfish. You think you're the only one with problems? You need to grow up, Annemarie. We're not in elementary school anymore."

"Me? I'm not the one who's playing house with Hugh. Yeah, sneaking around with your junior high boyfriend is real grown up. You wouldn't know the first thing about growing up!" I'm yelling now. "You have no idea! You don't even have your period!"

Elaine is trembling as she walks out the door. Breathing

hard, I fall back onto my bed and lie there. I'm trembling, too. I've lost my last friend, my best friend.

I stay in my room for the rest of the afternoon. I just read.

Near dinnertime I look out my window and see Mark on his bike, circling the block slowly. Around sunset I look out again, and there he is, inspecting a bike tire in front of my yard. He's waiting for me. But I won't be coming out. Let him suffer out there in the cold. I hope his guilt gobbles him up. I hope he feels like a nothing the same way I do.

chapter 44

When I get to school, Jack is leaning against my locker. "Hey, Einstein," he says. He's the last person I want to see. Besides Mark of course. Hate Mark.

"Hey." I set my book bag on the floor, and then watch as he turns the combination on my lock. He opens the locker door, hands me my English notebook, and turns back to me.

"So look—"

"How—how'd you know my combination?"

He rolls his eyes. "I know I'm not a genius like you, but give me a little credit, Annemarie. I've seen you open your locker enough times to know your combination. So—"

"What are you doing here, anyway? I thought you got suspended."

"Are you gonna let me finish a sentence?"

"Oh, sorry," I say. "Well, what do you want then?"

Funny how I never noticed he has green eyes.

He says, "I'm here to pick up my assignments. Hey, are you mad at me or something?"

"Yup." I slam my locker door shut and walk away. I don't have to turn around to know that he's watching me go.

chapter 45

Losing a boy best friend is one thing, but losing a girl best friend, your true best friend, is a whole different story. It's like losing a rib. There's something missing inside of you that you didn't even realize was there, and it makes it hard to breathe.

At school Elaine won't even look at me. I keep thinking, if she'll just look at me, everything will be okay. Our eyes will meet, and we'll both smile sheepishly. But when we pass each other in the halls, she doesn't look at me; she looks right through me. I eat lunch by myself in the girl's bathroom. It's the last day of school before Christmas break, and I should be happy. Instead, I've never felt so alone.

When I get on the bus at the end of the day, I'm not expecting to see Elaine, but there she is—sitting in our old seat. Alone, perched at the edge, as if to say Don't sit by me, don't even think it. When I walk by, she doesn't look my way. I'm not brave enough to sit next to her. Instead I sit behind her.

The bus starts moving, and soon we're riding along. I just sit there, staring at the back of her head.

To the back of her head, I say, "Where's Hugh?"

Elaine doesn't turn around. "Orthodontist appointment. He's getting braces."

"His teeth seem all right to me."

"He has an underbite." She turns around and looks at me then. "You know, he's not the only thing I think about."

Swallowing, I say, "I know."

"What you said to me was mean."

"I know. And I'm sorry."

She nods and turns back around, and I feel like I could cry. Then, slowly, she scoots over, closer to the window. Making room for me.

I pick up my book bag and move up to her seat. Neither of us says anything at first, but then Elaine says, "Annemarie, my life's not perfect either."

"Sure it is," I say. "Well, I mean, it's not *perfect*, but it's close. Your parents like each other. You're pretty. Boys like you."

Shaking her head, she says, "All of that isn't as easy as you think. Being here, in Clementon, hasn't been easy. Honestly, it sucks a lot of the time. It's harder than I expected. . . . And, Annemarie, you *are* pretty. I wish you could see that."

"Ha."

"Do you know how many times I've wished I look like you?"

Bewildered, I say, "Why would you want to look like me?"

"Think about it, Annemarie. I'm the only Korean American at our school. I'm the only Asian at our school."

"So?"

"So you have no idea how hard that is."

"But you're popular; everyone likes you."

Elaine shrugs. "It doesn't mean anything. They could have hated me just as easily. People will love you or hate you for being different, but who's to say which way it'll go? You never know. It's completely arbitrary. And anyway, it's not like no one's ever called me names."

I suck my breath in. "Like what?"

"Like 'chink.'" She says this word like it is nothing, like it can't hurt her, but I can see that it does, that it has.

"Oh. I'm sorry." I am sorry too, sorry that my Clementon, the place I call home, could be as mean as people say. I knew it wasn't perfect, but I guess I never dwelled too long on the why, or the how. I never thought how it must be for Elaine. Here I was thinking she had it so easy.

"Don't be sorry. Don't you get it? That's why me and you are special."

I don't get it. "What do you mean?"

Elaine says, "We're different. You like me for me, and I like you for you. The rest of it's all a bunch of crap."

"Yeah," I say. "It is."

Walking home from the bus stop, I see Mrs. Findley picking up the mail. I feel a funny clutch in my stomach, and I'm hoping she won't see me so I can go home without speaking to her. I keep my head low, walking fast.

But she does see me. "Annemarie!" she calls. She waves at me.

I look up like, who, me? "Hi, Mrs. Findley!" I call back, but I don't slow down.

"Come over here a minute!"

I trudge over to their mailbox. It's a good thing Mark had to stay after school for the Student Council Christmas party today. Otherwise I would have kept right on walking.

Mrs. Findley opens her arms and gives me a hug. She's wearing her thick lumberman's kind of coat, red plaid on the inside. She smells like cinnamon and wood chips. "How come I haven't seen you in so long?" she says.

"Oh, you know. I've been busy with school and stuff."

"Still, I wish I could've taken pictures of you and Mark for your first dance. I would have loved to have seen you all dressed up. I know you must have been so lovely," she says, putting both hands on my cheeks. "Did you have a nice time?"

Looking away, I say, "Mm-hmm, real nice."

"Honey, is something wrong?" Mrs. Findley's brow furrows. "Have you and Mark had a falling out?"

"Why would you think that?"

"Well, you haven't been by the house in such a long time. And Mark did mention something . . ." Her voice trails off.

I'm dying to know what he said, but I don't ask. Instead I say nothing; I just keep my lips clamped shut.

"Well, I know you two will work it out," Mrs. Findley says at last. "How about you come over for dinner tonight? I'll make spaghetti. We can bake those Christmas cookies you love, the pecan crescents."

I smile. "I wish I could, but I have to be at home for dinner tonight."

She nods. "All right, then. You know you're always welcome."

"I know," I say. Then I walk home.

chapter 46

The next day I'm finally ready to see Mark. The sun's just beginning to set, and I go out to the front porch and wait. Meeks waits with me. I think he misses Mark.

The sun's dipping away when Mark comes down my street on his bike. He slows down when he sees me, and then he rides down my driveway. "Sic him," I whisper to Meeks, who brightens when he sees Mark. Meeks, the lousy traitor, bounds over to Mark and starts licking his knees.

"Hey," Mark says. He sets his bike down on the ground very carefully, taking an extra long time. He stoops low to pet Meeks and then faces me.

"What do you want?" I look straight ahead, straight past him.

"I came to say sorry," he says, and his voice cracks. First time I ever heard it crack. I wonder if it's been cracking all along, and I just never heard it. "I'm sorry for what I said at the dance. I didn't mean it."

"Yeah, you did." I look at him now, right in the eyes.

Mark looks back at me, and his eyes are watery and scared. He is about to cry. "No, really. I didn't mean it."

"Then why'd you say it?"

The corners of his lips turn down, and he thinks hard for a moment. That's what Mark does when he's thinking hard—he frowns. He stands there, thinking and looking puzzled, with his hands in his pockets. Then he says, "I don't know. I don't know why I said it, but I know I'm sorry."

I actually believe him. He really doesn't know. He doesn't know any more than I do. "Sorry isn't good enough. Sorry doesn't take away what you said. Sorry doesn't mean we can be friends again."

"I know, but . . ." He trails off. But nothing. He has nothing to say for himself.

"If you came over here thinking we could just go back to being friends the way we used to—"

That's what I hope he came over for, anyway. To beg that we could be BFF, best friends forever, like before. And

I'll say no, and Mark'll keep begging, and then I'll give in, because that's what we do.

"No, I know we can't."

"You do?"

"Yeah. I just came to say I'm sorry."

"Oh."

Mark stands there, with the sun setting against his back. Then he pulls his bike up off the ground and starts to ride back down my driveway.

I don't say good-bye, and neither does he.

chapter 47

All day at school I wondered if Daddy was coming home. That last fight was so bad, I wondered if it was the final straw. I wondered if it meant the *D* word was right around the corner. I didn't want to ask Mama. But Celia said not to worry; he'd be there. I hope she's right. She usually is.

As the clock ticks closer to dinnertime, Mama stays in her room. The door is shut. Celia's door is shut too. I guess it's up to me to cook supper.

I'm stirring a pot of macaroni when Daddy strides through the back door. "Hey, Shug," he says, setting his briefcase on the floor. "What's cookin'?"

He winks at me, and I can't remember the last time I was this happy to see him. Dropping the wooden spoon on the counter, I run over to him, my daddy. I breathe in his daddy smell and hug him tight. "Hey, what's all this for?" he says, smiling and chucking my chin.

"Nothing," I say, backing away. "Macaroni's cooking. Mama's upstairs. So's Celia."

Loosening his tie, Daddy says, "Well, I'll just go get washed up before supper then." He leaves the kitchen, and as I lean against the counter, my happiness starts to fade away. I wonder what happens next. Did he come home just so he could announce he was leaving for good? Could Mairi's mother be right? I always thought that I wouldn't mind if Mama and Daddy got divorced, not truly. I thought, well, maybe it'll be better that way, maybe some people just aren't meant to be together. But faced with the possibility, I choose together. I choose us. Even if it is all just pretend.

The four of us sit around the kitchen table, the first time in a long time. For once, there's no wineglass in Mama's hand, just iced tea. For once, Celia isn't rushing off to meet Park, or Margaret, or anybody that isn't us. For once, Daddy is here.

I keep waiting for Daddy to make his announcement, but it never comes. We eat dinner. There's not a lot of talk, we just eat.

It's around 9:30 p.m. when the doorbell rings. Mama

and Daddy are watching TV in the den, Celia's in her room, and I'm doing my homework at the dining room table. Part of me is still waiting for that announcement.

We all look at one another when we hear the door, like, who the heck could that be? We're not used to late-night visitors. Neither of them make a move from the couch, and sighing loudly, I get up. As I head for the front door, I see Mama put her head in Daddy's lap, and I feel more okay than I have in a long time.

I open the door. It's Jack. He says, "Can you come outside for a minute?"

"Uh, yeah, I guess." I grab my puffy jacket from the coat hook and zip into it. Closing the door, I holler, "It's for me!" Not that anybody cares.

We sit down on the front steps. It's pitch black outside, and the sky is swimming with stars. It's nights like these that make you realize you're sitting on a planet. We're on a planet, in an ocean of stars. They're so close you could reach out and grab one, put it in your pocket for later. If I had a fishing net, I'd take them all. I'd line my ceiling with them.

Jack pulls a roll of cherry Life Savers out of his pocket. He takes the one on top, then gives me the next one. If you didn't know him better, you might think he was being rude, taking the first one and all. But I knew that he took the top piece because the top piece of a roll of Life Savers is always linty and fuzzy from being in your pocket. The ones in the middle are the good ones. I pop that good middle one in my mouth.

He says, "You mad at me for getting out-of-school suspension?"

Clicking the Life Saver on my teeth, I say, "Well, yeah."

"You still mad at me for getting into a fight with Mark?"

"Yup."

"'Cause you like him."

"No, because it was stupid. Why'd you have to go and get in trouble again?"

"I don't know." He clears his throat. "The thing is, I'm gonna have to go and live with my dad for a while. I'm gonna leave after Christmas. My mom's actually going through with it. She already called him and everything."

"Oh."

"Yeah."

"For how long?"

"Don't know."

"Oh." I bite my lip. I don't know how to say this next part. "Are you scared?"

He doesn't say anything for a minute. "No. I mean, I still hate him. I still hate what he did to my mom. But, I don't know . . . I saw him last month. He actually came to see me.

He seems . . . better. I don't know how to explain it."

I say, "You don't have to."

We sit there, not talking, just staring up at the sky. How many times had Mark and I sat together, just like this, on a night just like this one, saying nothing, just sharing the silence? Too many to count. It's funny, but this night feels different than all those other nights. Like Jack and I aren't just sharing the silence, but we're waiting for something.

Jack's got that look on his face, the look he gets when he's standing on the pitcher's mound. That summer we played softball in the park, he was always the pitcher, and he always had the same expression on his face right before he hit you with a real doozy. That's how he looks right now. Nervous. He looks nervous. Then he says, "I'm sorry about the way things turned out."

"Yeah?"

"Yeah." A long pause, and then, "Mark can be such a jerk sometimes."

"Sometimes. He's not really like that though." I feel oddly defensive.

He doesn't look at me. "You still like him, even after . . . ?"

"No . . ." I don't look at him either. "But he's still my friend, even after."

"Oh."

I'm nervous, really really nervous. I've got the whole rest of my life for kissing. I don't even want him to kiss me. Maybe I do want him to kiss me, but only a little bit. Not enough to let him.

He leans a bit closer and then turns away. Out of the corner of my eye, I watch him. His profile is soft in the dark like this—I want to touch the curve of his cheek, just to see what it feels like. Does it feel like mine? Where did that thought even come from? Certainly not from me. I don't care what his cheek feels like. Oily, probably.

But it doesn't look oily. It looks clean.

I rest my left hand on my knee. It just sits there, naked and alone. I wish he'd cover it with his hand. Cover me up. Hold my hand. Do something. He's such a jerk; he's just sitting there doing nothing.

I close my eyes and will something to happen. Just to see. Maybe I'll hate it. But maybe I won't.

He doesn't kiss me. Instead he touches the scar on my cheek, just for a second. So quick it almost didn't happen. But it did happen. His fingers felt light and warm on my face. "I'm sorry about that too," he says, and his voice sounds strange.

I stop breathing, I think. Then he says, "I'm sorry for,

you know, pulling your hair out that one time too. I just wanted to see what it looked like down."

That's when I kiss him. Without thinking, I just lean forward and do it. In that moment all I hear are the crickets and my heartbeat. The kiss lasts about four seconds, maybe five. Not what I thought it'd be like at all. Soft and warm and sort of surprising. He tastes like candy. I'll remember this taste for the rest of my life. I thought my first kiss would taste like a cherry Popsicle. Cherry Life Savers are okay too. Better, maybe.

I break away, swallow hard, and say, "Something to remember me by." All I can think is, please don't make a joke out of this. Don't make a joke of me.

He doesn't. He just grins crookedly and says, "How could I forget?" Then he stands up and shoves his hands into his pockets. "Guess I'd better go. See ya, Annemarie."

"See ya." He walks down the steps, and I watch his sneakers move along the rocky pavement and away from me.

I wait until he's at the end of the driveway before I let myself shout, "You better write me! I wanna know that all my hard work wasn't for nothing!"

He turns around and yells back, "Keep dreaming, Einstein!" But he's smiling.

I'm smiling too. He'll write. I know he will.

Real life. Real you.

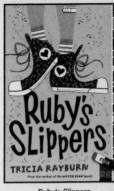

Ruby's Slippers

Don't miss
any of these
terrific
Aladdin Mix
books.

Home Sweet Drama

This Is Me From Now On

Devon Delaney Should
Totally Know Better

Front Page Face-Off

Nice and Mean

Jenny Han—Han like Hawn, Goldie; or Han Solo—was born and raised in Richmond, Virginia. She graduated from the University of North Carolina at Chapel Hill (Go Carolina!) and earned an MFA in writing for children at New School University. She enjoys cupcakes, Scrabble, and hip-hop music. She lives in New York City. This is her first novel. Visit Jenny at www.jennyhanwrites.com.